MW00947707

Wilhelm Tell

Friedrich Schiller

Copyright © 2017 Okitoks Press

All rights reserved.

ISBN: 1983776165

ISBN-13: 978-1983776168

Table of Contents

DRAMATIS PERSONAE.

HERMANN GESSLER, Governor of Schwytz and Uri.
WERNER, Baron of Attinghausen, free noble of Switzerland.
ULRICH VON RUDENZ, his Nephew.

WERNER STAUFFACHER, |
CONRAD HUNN, |
HANS AUF DER MAUER, |
JORG IM HOFE, | People of Schwytz.
ULRICH DER SCHMIDT, |
JOST VON WEILER, |
ITEL REDING, |

WALTER FURST, |
WILHELM TELL, |
ROSSELMANN, the Priest, |
PETERMANN, Sacristan, | People of Uri.
KUONI, Herdsman, |
WERNI, Huntsman, |
RUODI, Fisherman, |

ARNOLD OF MELCHTHAL, |
CONRAD BAUMGARTEN, |
MEYER VON SARNEN, |
STRUTH VON WINKELRIED, | People of Unterwald.
KLAUS VON DER FLUE, |
BURKHART AM BUHEL, |
ARNOLD VON SEWA, |

PFEIFFER OF LUCERNE.
KUNZ OF GERSAU.
JENNI, Fisherman's Son.
SEPPI, Herdsman's Son.
GERTRUDE, Stauffacher's Wife.
HEDWIG, Wife of Tell, daughter of Furst.
BERTHA OF BRUNECK, a rich heiress.

ARMGART, |
MECHTHILD, | Peasant women.
ELSBETH, |
HILDEGARD, |

WALTER, | Tell's sons.
WILHELM, |

FRIESSHARDT, | Soldiers.
LEUTHOLD, |

RUDOLPH DER HARRAS, Gessler's master of the horse.
JOHANNES PARRICIDA, Duke of Suabia.
STUSSI, Overseer.
THE MAYOR OF URI.
A COURIER.
MASTER STONEMASON, COMPANIONS, AND WORKMEN.
TASKMASTER.
A CRIER.
MONKS OF THE ORDER OF CHARITY.
HORSEMEN OF GESSLER AND LANDENBERG.
MANY PEASANTS; MEN AND WOMEN FROM THE WALDSTETTEN.

WILHELM TELL.

ACT I.

SCENE I.

A high, rocky shore of the lake of Lucerne opposite Schwytz.
The lake makes a bend into the land; a hut stands at a short
distance from the shore; the fisher boy is rowing about in his
boat. Beyond the lake are seen the green meadows, the hamlets,
and arms of Schwytz, lying in the clear sunshine. On the left
are observed the peaks of the Hacken, surrounded with clouds; to
the right, and in the remote distance, appear the Glaciers. The
Ranz des Vaches, and the tinkling of cattle-bells, continue for
some time after the rising of the curtain.

4

FISHER BOY (sings in his boat).
Melody of the Ranz des Vaches.

    The clear, smiling lake wooed to bathe in its deep,
    A boy on its green shore had laid him to sleep;
        Then heard he a melody
        Flowing and soft,
        And sweet, as when angels
        Are singing aloft.
    And as thrilling with pleasure he wakes from his rest,
    The waters are murmuring over his breast;
        And a voice from the deep cries,
        "With me thou must go,
        I charm the young shepherd,
        I lure him below."

HERDSMAN (on the mountains).
Air.—Variation of the Ranz des Vaches.

        Farewell, ye green meadows,
        Farewell, sunny shore,
        The herdsman must leave you,
        The summer is o'er.
   We go to the hills, but you'll see us again,
    When the cuckoo is calling, and wood-notes are gay,
   When flowerets are blooming in dingle and plain,
   And the brooks sparkle up in the sunshine of May.
        Farewell, ye green meadows,
        Farewell, sunny shore,
        The herdsman must leave you,
        The summer is o'er.

CHAMOIS HUNTER (appearing on the top of a cliff).
Second Variation of the Ranz des Vaches.

    On the heights peals the thunder, and trembles the bridge,
    The huntsman bounds on by the dizzying ridge,
        Undaunted he hies him
        O'er ice-covered wild,
        Where leaf never budded,
        Nor spring ever smiled;
    And beneath him an ocean of mist, where his eye
    No longer the dwellings of man can espy;
        Through the parting clouds only
        The earth can be seen,
        Far down 'neath the vapor

The meadows of green.

[A change comes over the landscape. A rumbling, cracking
noise is heard among the mountains. Shadows of clouds sweep
across the scene.

[RUODI, the fisherman, comes out of his cottage. WERNI, the
huntsman, descends from the rocks. KUONI, the shepherd, enters,
with a milk pail on his shoulders, followed by SERPI, his assistant.

RUODI.
Bestir thee, Jenni, haul the boat on shore.
The grizzly Vale-king 1 comes, the glaciers moan,
The lofty Mytenstein 2 draws on his hood,
And from the Stormcleft chilly blows the wind;
The storm will burst before we are prepared.

KUONI.
'Twill rain ere long; my sheep browse eagerly,
And Watcher there is scraping up the earth.

WERNI.
The fish are leaping, and the water-hen
Dives up and down. A storm is coming on.

KUONI (to his boy).
Look, Seppi, if the cattle are not straying.

SEPPI. There goes brown Liesel, I can hear her bells.

KUONI.
Then all are safe; she ever ranges farthest.

RUODI.
You've a fine yoke of bells there, master herdsman.

WERNI.
And likely cattle, too. Are they your own?

KUONI.
I'm not so rich. They are the noble lord's
Of Attinghaus, and trusted to my care.

RUODI.
How gracefully yon heifer bears her ribbon!

KUONI.
Ay, well she knows she's leader of the herd,
And, take it from her, she'd refuse to feed.

RUODI.
You're joking now. A beast devoid of reason.

WERNI.
That's easy said. But beasts have reason too—
And that we know, we men that hunt the chamois.
They never turn to feed—sagacious creatures!
Till they have placed a sentinel ahead,
Who pricks his ears whenever we approach,
And gives alarm with clear and piercing pipe.

RUODI (to the shepherd).
Are you for home?

KUONI.
　　　　The Alp is grazed quite bare.

WERNI.
A safe return, my friend!

KUONI.
　　　　The same to you?
Men come not always back from tracks like yours.

RUODI.
But who comes here, running at topmost speed?

WERNI.
I know the man; 'tis Baumgart of Alzellen.

CONRAD BAUMGARTEN (rushing in breathless).
For God's sake, ferryman, your boat!

RUODI.
　　　　How now?
Why all this haste?

BAUMGARTEN.
　　　　Cast off! My life's at stake!
Set me across!

KUONI.

Why, what's the matter, friend?

WERNI.
Who are pursuing you? First tell us that.

BAUMGARTEN (to the fisherman).
Quick, quick, even now they're close upon my heels!
The viceroy's horsemen are in hot pursuit!
I'm a lost man should they lay hands upon me.

RUODI.
Why are the troopers in pursuit of you?

BAUMGARTEN.
First save my life and then I'll tell you all.

WERNI.
There's blood upon your garments—how is this?

BAUMGARTEN.
The imperial seneschal, who dwelt at Rossberg.

KUONI.
How! What! The Wolfshot? 3 Is it he pursues you?

BAUMGARTEN.
He'll ne'er hunt man again; I've settled him.

ALL (starting back).
Now, God forgive you, what is this you've done!

BAUMGARTEN.
What every free man in my place had done.
I have but used mine own good household right
'Gainst him that would have wronged my wife—my honor.

KUONI.
And has he wronged you in your honor, then?

BAUMGARTEN.
That he did not fulfil his foul desire
Is due to God and to my trusty axe.

WERNI.
You've cleft his skull, then, have you, with your axe?

KUONI.
Oh, tell us all! You've time enough, before
The boat can be unfastened from its moorings.

BAUMGARTEN.
When I was in the forest, felling timber,
My wife came running out in mortal fear:
"The seneschal," she said, "was in my house,
Had ordered her to get a bath prepared,
And thereupon had taken unseemly freedoms,
From which she rid herself and flew to me."
Armed as I was I sought him, and my axe
Has given his bath a bloody benediction.

WERNI.
And you did well; no man can blame the deed.

KUONI.
The tyrant! Now he has his just reward!
We men of Unterwald have owed it long.

BAUMGARTEN.
The deed got wind, and now they're in pursuit.
Heavens! whilst we speak, the time is flying fast.

[It begins to thunder.

KUONI.
Quick, ferrymen, and set the good man over.

RUODI.
Impossible! a storm is close at hand,
Wait till it pass! You must.

BAUMGARTEN.
       Almighty heavens!
I cannot wait; the least delay is death.

KUONI (to the fisherman).
Push out. God with you! We should help our neighbors;
The like misfortune may betide us all.

[Thunder and the roaring of the wind.

RUODI.
The south wind's up! 4 See how the lake is rising!

9

I cannot steer against both storm and wave.

BAUMGARTEN (clasping him by the knees).
God so help you, as now you pity me!

WERNI.
His life's at stake. Have pity on him, man!

KUONI.
He is a father: has a wife and children.

   [Repeated peals of thunder.

RUODI.
What! and have I not, then, a life to lose,
A wife and child at home as well as he?
See, how the breakers foam, and toss, and whirl,
And the lake eddies up from all its depths!
Right gladly would I save the worthy man,
But 'tis impossible, as you must see.

BAUMGARTEN (still kneeling).
Then must I fall into the tyrant's hands,
And with the port of safety close in sight!
Yonder it lies! My eyes can measure it,
My very voice can echo to its shores.
There is the boat to carry me across,
Yet must I lie here helpless and forlorn.

KUONI.
Look! who comes here?

RUODI.
      'Tis Tell, brave Tell, of Buerglen. 5

   [Enter TELL, with a crossbow.

TELL.
Who is the man that here implores for aid?

KUONI.
He is from Alzellen, and to guard his honor
From touch of foulest shame, has slain the Wolfshot!
The imperial seneschal, who dwelt at Rossberg.
The viceroy's troopers are upon his heels;
He begs the boatman here to take him over,

10

But he, in terror of the storm, refuses.

RUODI.
Well, there is Tell can steer as well as I.
He'll be my judge, if it be possible.

[Violent peals of thunder—the lake becomes more tempestuous.

Am I to plunge into the jaws of hell?
I should be mad to dare the desperate act.

TELL.
The brave man thinks upon himself the last.
Put trust in God, and help him in his need!

RUODI.
Safe in the port, 'tis easy to advise.
There is the boat, and there the lake! Try you!

TELL.
The lake may pity, but the viceroy will not.
Come, venture, man!

SHEPHERD and **HUNTSMAN.**
Oh, save him! save him! save him!

RUODI.
Though 'twere my brother, or my darling child,
I would not go. It is St. Simon's day,
The lake is up, and calling for its victim.

TELL.
Naught's to be done with idle talking here.
Time presses on—the man must be assisted.
Say, boatman, will you venture?

RUODI.
No; not I.

TELL.
In God's name, then, give me the boat! I will
With my poor strength, see what is to be done!

KUONI.
Ha, noble Tell!

WERNI.

That's like a gallant huntsman!

BAUMGARTEN.

You are my angel, my preserver, Tell.

TELL.

I may preserve you from the viceroy's power
But from the tempest's rage another must.
Yet you had better fall into God's hands,
Than into those of men.
　　[To the herdsman.
　　　　　Herdsman, do thou
Console my wife, should aught of ill befall me.
I do but what I may not leave undone.

　　[He leaps into the boat.

KUONI (to the fisherman).

A pretty man to be a boatman, truly!
What Tell could risk you dared not venture on.

RUODI.

Far better men than I would not ape Tell.
There does not live his fellow 'mong the mountains.

WERNI (who has ascended a rock).

He pushes off. God help thee now, brave sailor!
Look how his bark is reeling on the waves!

KUONI (on the shore).

The surge has swept clean over it. And now
'Tis out of sight. Yet stay, there 'tis again
Stoutly he stems the breakers, noble fellow!

SEPPI.

Here come the troopers hard as they can ride!

KUONI.

Heavens! so they do! Why, that was help, indeed.

　　[Enter a troop of horsemen.

FIRST HORSEMAN.

Give up the murderer! You have him here!

12

SECOND HORSEMAN.
This way he came! 'Tis useless to conceal him!

RUODI and **KUONI.**
Whom do you mean?

FIRST HORSEMAN (discovering the boat).
    The devil! What do I see?

WERNI (from above).
Is't he in yonder boat ye seek? Ride on,
If you lay to, you may o'ertake him yet.

SECOND HORSEMAN.
Curse on you, he's escaped!

FIRST HORSEMAN (to the shepherd and fisherman).
    You helped him off,
And you shall pay for it. Fall on their herds!
Down with the cottage! burn it! beat it down!

       [They rush off.

SEPPI (hurrying after them).
Oh, my poor lambs!

KUONI (following him).
    Unhappy me, my herds!

WERNI.
The tyrants!

RUODI (wringing his hands).
    Righteous Heaven! Oh, when will come
Deliverance to this devoted land?

       [Exeunt severally.

SCENE II.

A lime-tree in front of STAUFFACHER'S house at Steinen,
in Schwytz, upon the public road, near a bridge.

13

WERNER STAUFFACHER and PFEIFFER, of Lucerne, enter into conversation.

PFEIFFER.
Ay, ay, friend Stauffacher, as I have said,
Swear not to Austria, if you can help it.
Hold by the empire stoutly as of yore,
And God preserve you in your ancient freedom!

[Presses his hand warmly and is going.

STAUFFACHER.
Wait till my mistress comes. Now do! You are
My guest in Schwytz—I in Lucerne am yours.

PFEIFFER.
Thanks! thanks! But I must reach Gersau to-day.
Whatever grievances your rulers' pride
And grasping avarice may yet inflict,
Bear them in patience—soon a change may come.
Another emperor may mount the throne.
But Austria's once, and you are hers forever.

[Exit.

[STAUFEACHER sits down sorrowfully upon a bench
under the lime tree. Gertrude, his wife, enters,
and finds him in this posture. She places herself
near him, and looks at him for some time in silence.

GERTRUDE.
So sad, my love! I scarcely know thee now.
For many a day in silence I have marked
A moody sorrow furrowing thy brow.
Some silent grief is weighing on thy heart;
Trust it to me. I am thy faithful wife,
And I demand my half of all thy cares.

[STAUFFACHER gives her his hand and is silent.

Tell me what can oppress thy spirits thus?
Thy toil is blest—the world goes well with thee—
Our barns are full—our cattle many a score;
Our handsome team of sleek and well-fed steeds,
Brought from the mountain pastures safely home,

14

To winter in their comfortable stalls.
There stands thy house—no nobleman's more fair!
'Tis newly built with timber of the best,
All grooved and fitted with the nicest skill;
Its many glistening windows tell of comfort!
'Tis quartered o'er with scutcheons of all hues,
And proverbs sage, which passing travellers
Linger to read, and ponder o'er their meaning.

STAUFFACHER.
The house is strongly built, and handsomely,
But, ah! the ground on which we built it totters.

GERTRUDE.
Tell me, dear Werner, what you mean by that?

STAUFFACHER.
No later since than yesterday, I sat
Beneath this linden, thinking with delight,
How fairly all was finished, when from Kuessnacht
The viceroy and his men came riding by.
Before this house he halted in surprise:
At once I rose, and, as beseemed his rank,
Advanced respectfully to greet the lord,
To whom the emperor delegates his power,
As judge supreme within our Canton here.
"Who is the owner of this house?" he asked,
With mischief in his thoughts, for well he knew.
With prompt decision, thus I answered him:
"The emperor, your grace—my lord and yours,
And held by one in fief." On this he answered,
"I am the emperor's viceregent here,
And will not that each peasant churl should build
At his own pleasure, bearing him as freely
As though he were the master in the land.
I shall make bold to put a stop to this!"
So saying he, with menaces, rode off,
And left me musing, with a heavy heart,
On the fell purpose that his words betrayed.

GERTRUDE.
Mine own dear lord and husband! Wilt thou take
A word of honest counsel from thy wife?
I boast to be the noble Iberg's child,
A man of wide experience. Many a time,
As we sat spinning in the winter nights,

15

My sisters and myself, the people's chiefs
Were wont to gather round our father's hearth,
To read the old imperial charters, and
To hold sage converse on the country's weal.
Then heedfully I listened, marking well
What or the wise men thought, or good man wished,
And garnered up their wisdom in my heart.
Hear then, and mark me well; for thou wilt see,
I long have known the grief that weighs thee down.
The viceroy hates thee, fain would injure thee,
For thou hast crossed his wish to bend the Swiss
In homage to this upstart house of princes,
And kept them stanch, like their good sires of old,
In true allegiance to the empire. Say.
Is't not so, Werner? Tell nee, am I wrong?

STAUFFACHER.
'Tis even so. For this doth Gessler hate me.

GERTRUDE.
He burns with envy, too, to see thee living
Happy and free on thy inheritance,
For he has none. From the emperor himself
Thou holdest in fief the lands thy fathers left thee.
There's not a prince in the empire that can show
A better title to his heritage;
For thou hast over thee no lord but one,
And he the mightiest of all Christian kings.
Gessler, we know, is but a younger son,
His only wealth the knightly cloak he wears;
He therefore views an honest man's good fortune
With a malignant and a jealous eye.
Long has he sworn to compass thy destruction
As yet thou art uninjured. Wilt thou wait
Till he may safely give his malice scope?
A wise man would anticipate the blow.

STAUFFACHER.
What's to be done?

GERTRUDE.
    Now hear what I advise.
Thou knowest well, how here with us in Schwytz,
All worthy men are groaning underneath
This Gessler's grasping, grinding tyranny.
Doubt not the men of Unterwald as well,

And Uri, too, are chafing like ourselves,
At this oppressive and heart-wearying yoke.
For there, across the lake, the Landenberg
Wields the same iron rule as Gessler here—
No fishing-boat comes over to our side
But brings the tidings of some new encroachment,
Some outrage fresh, more grievous than the last.
Then it were well that some of you—true men—
Men sound at heart, should secretly devise
How best to shake this hateful thraldom off.
Well do I know that God would not desert you,
But lend his favor to the righteous cause.
Hast thou no friend in Uri, say, to whom
Thou frankly may'st unbosom all thy thoughts?

STAUFFACHER.
I know full many a gallant fellow there,
And nobles, too,—great men, of high repute,
In whom I can repose unbounded trust.

      [Rising.

Wife! What a storm of wild and perilous thoughts
Hast thou stirred up within my tranquil breast?
The darkest musings of my bosom thou
Hast dragged to light, and placed them full before me,
And what I scarce dared harbor e'en in thought,
Thou speakest plainly out, with fearless tongue.
But hast thou weighed well what thou urgest thus?
Discord will come, and the fierce clang of arms,
To scare this valley's long unbroken peace,
If we, a feeble shepherd race, shall dare
Him to the fight that lords it o'er the world.
Even now they only wait some fair pretext
For setting loose their savage warrior hordes,
To scourge and ravage this devoted land,
To lord it o'er us with the victor's rights,
And 'neath the show of lawful chastisement,
Despoil us of our chartered liberties.

GERTRUDE.
You, too, are men; can wield a battle-axe
As well as they. God ne'er deserts the brave.

STAUFFACHER.
Oh wife! a horrid, ruthless fiend is war,

17

That strikes at once the shepherd and his flock.

GERTRUDE.
Whate'er great heaven inflicts we must endure;
No heart of noble temper brooks injustice.

STAUFFACHER.
This house—thy pride—war, unrelenting war,
Will burn it down.

GERTRUDE.
      And did I think this heart
Enslaved and fettered to the things of earth,
With my own hand I'd hurl the kindling torch.

STAUFFACHER.
Thou hast faith in human kindness, wife; but war
Spares not the tender infant in its cradle.

GERTRUDE.
There is a friend to innocence in heaven
Look forward, Werner—not behind you, now!

STAUFFACHER.
We men may perish bravely, sword in hand;
But oh, what fate, my Gertrude, may be thine?

GERTRUDE.
None are so weak, but one last choice is left.
A spring from yonder bridge, and I am free!

STAUFFACHER (embracing her).
Well may he fight for hearth and home that clasps
A heart so rare as thine against his own!
What are the hosts of emperors to him!
Gertrude, farewell! I will to Uri straight.
There lives my worthy comrade, Walter Furst,
His thoughts and mine upon these times are one.
There, too, resides the noble Banneret
Of Attinghaus. High though of blood he be,
He loves the people, honors their old customs.
With both of these I will take counsel how
To rid us bravely of our country's foe.
Farewell! and while I am away, bear thou
A watchful eye in management at home.
The pilgrim journeying to the house of God,

And pious monk, collecting for his cloister,
To these give liberally from purse and garner.
Stauffacher's house would not be hid. Right out
Upon the public way it stands, and offers
To all that pass an hospitable roof.

[While they are retiring, TELL enters with BAUMGARTEN.

TELL.
Now, then, you have no further need of me.
Enter yon house. 'Tis Werner Stauffacher's,
A man that is a father to distress.
See, there he is himself! Come, follow me.

[They retire up. Scene changes.

SCENE III.

A common near Altdorf. On an eminence in the background a castle
in progress of erection, and so far advanced that the outline of the
whole may be distinguished. The back part is finished; men are
working at the front. Scaffolding, on which the workmen are going
up and down. A slater is seen upon the highest part of the roof.—
All is bustle and activity.

TASKMASTER, MASON, WORKMEN, and LABORERS.

TASKMASTER (with a stick, urging on the workmen).
Up, up! You've rested long enough. To work!
The stones here, now the mortar, and the lime!
And let his lordship see the work advanced
When next he comes. These fellows crawl like snails!

[To two laborers with loads.

What! call ye that a load? Go, double it.
Is this the way ye earn your wages, laggards?

FIRST WORKMAN.
'Tis very hard that we must bear the stones,
To make a keep and dungeon for ourselves!

TASKMASTER.
What's that you mutter? 'Tis a worthless race,
And fit for nothing but to milk their cows,
And saunter idly up and down the mountains.

OLD MAN (sinks down exhausted).
I can no more.

TASKMASTER (shaking him).
　　Up, up, old man, to work!

FIRST WORKMAN.
Have you no bowels of compassion, thus
To press so hard upon a poor old man,
That scarce can drag his feeble limbs along?

MASTER MASON and **WORKMEN.**
Shame, shame upon you—shame! It cries to heaven!

TASKMASTER.
Mind your own business. I but do my duty.

FIRST WORKMAN.
Pray, master, what's to be the name of this
Same castle when 'tis built?

TASKMASTER.
　　　The keep of Uri;
For by it we shall keep you in subjection.

WORKMEN.
The keep of Uri.

TASKMASTER.
　　Well, why laugh at that?

SECOND WORKMAN.
So you'll keep Uri with this paltry place!

FIRST WORKMAN.
How many molehills such as that must first
Be piled above each other ere you make
A mountain equal to the least in Uri?

　　[TASKMASTER retires up the stage.

MASTER MASON.
I'll drown the mallet in the deepest lake,
That served my hand on this accursed pile.

[Enter TELL and STAUFFACHER.

STAUFFACHER.
Oh, that I had not lived to see this sight!

TELL.
Here 'tis not good to be. Let us proceed.

STAUFFACHER.
Am I in Uri, in the land of freedom?

MASTER MASON.
Oh, sir, if you could only see the vaults
Beneath these towers. The man that tenants them
Will never hear the cock crow more.

STAUFFACHER.
       O God!

MASTER MASON.
Look at these ramparts and these buttresses,
That seem as they were built to last forever.

TELL.
Hands can destroy whatever hands have reared.

[Pointing to the mountains.

That house of freedom God hath built for us.

[A drum is heard. People enter bearing a cap upon a
pole, followed by a crier. Women and children thronging
tumultuously after them.

FIRST WORKMAN.
What means the drum? Give heed!

MASTER MASON.
      Why here's a mumming!
And look, the cap,—what can they mean by that?

CRIER.

In the emperor's name, give ear!

WORKMEN.
        Hush! silence! hush!

CRIER.
Ye men of Uri, ye do see this cap!
It will be set upon a lofty pole
In Altdorf, in the market-place: and this
Is the lord governor's good will and pleasure,
The cap shall have like honor as himself,
And all shall reverence it with bended knee,
And head uncovered; thus the king will know
Who are his true and loyal subjects here:
His life and goods are forfeit to the crown,
That shall refuse obedience to the order.

[The people burst out into laughter. The drum beats,
and the procession passes on.

FIRST WORKMAN.
A strange device to fall upon, indeed!
Do reverence to a cap! a pretty farce!
Heard ever mortal anything like this?

MASTER MASON.
Down to a cap on bended knee, forsooth!
Rare jesting this with men of sober sense!

FIRST WORKMAN.
Nay, were it but the imperial crown, indeed!
But 'tis the cap of Austria! I've seen it
Hanging above the throne in Gessler's hall.

MASTER MASON.
The cap of Austria! Mark that! A snare
To get us into Austria's power, by heaven!

WORKMEN.
No freeborn man will stoop to such disgrace.

MASTER MASON.

Come—to our comrades, and advise with them!

[They retire up.

TELL (to STAUFFACHER).
You see how matters stand: Farewell, my friend!

STAUFFACHER.
Whither away? Oh, leave us not so soon.

TELL.
They look for me at home. So fare ye well.

STAUFFACHER.
My heart's so full, and has so much to tell you.

TELL.
Words will not make a heart that's heavy light.

STAUFFACHER.
Yet words may possibly conduct to deeds.

TELL.
All we can do is to endure in silence.

STAUFFACHER.
But shall we bear what is not to be borne?

TELL.
Impetuous rulers have the shortest reigns.
When the fierce south wind rises from his chasms,
Men cover up their fires, the ships in haste
Make for the harbor, and the mighty spirit
Sweeps o'er the earth, and leaves no trace behind.
Let every man live quietly at home;
Peace to the peaceful rarely is denied.

STAUFFACHER.
And is it thus you view our grievances?

TELL.
The serpent stings not till it is provoked.
Let them alone; they'll weary of themselves,
Whene'er they see we are not to be roused.

STAUFFACHER.

Much might be done—did we stand fast together.

TELL.
When the ship founders, he will best escape
Who seeks no other's safety but his own.

STAUFFACHER.
And you desert the common cause so coldly?

TELL.
A man can safely count but on himself!

STAUFFACHER.
Nay, even the weak grow strong by union.

TELL.
But the strong man is the strongest when alone.

STAUFFACHER.
Your country, then, cannot rely on you
If in despair she rise against her foes.

TELL.
Tell rescues the lost sheep from yawning gulfs:
Is he a man, then, to desert his friends?
Yet, whatsoe'er you do, spare me from council!
I was not born to ponder and select;
But when your course of action is resolved,
Then call on Tell; you shall not find him fail.

[Exeunt severally. A sudden tumult is heard around the scaffolding.

MASTER MASON (running in).
What's wrong?

FIRST WORKMAN (running forward).
The slater's fallen from the roof.

BERTHA (rushing in).
Is he dashed to pieces? Run—save him, help!
If help be possible, save him! Here is gold.

[Throws her trinkets among the people.

MASTER MASON.
Hence with your gold,—your universal charm,

And remedy for ill! When you have torn
Fathers from children, husbands from their wives,
And scattered woe and wail throughout the land,
You think with gold to compensate for all.
Hence! Till we saw you we were happy men;
With you came misery and dark despair.

BERTHA (to the TASKMASTER, who has returned).
Lives he?
  [TASKMASTER shakes his head.
   Ill-fated towers, with curses built,
And doomed with curses to be tenanted!

      [Exit.

SCENE IV.

  The House of WALTER FURST.
WALTER FURST and ARNOLD
  VON MELCHTHAL enter simultaneously at different sides.

MELCHTHAL.
Good Walter Furst.

FURST.
    If we should be surprised!
Stay where you are. We are beset with spies.

MELCHTHAL.
Have you no news for me from Unterwald?
What of my father? 'Tis not to be borne,
Thus to be pent up like a felon here!
What have I done of such a heinous stamp,
To skulk and hide me like a murderer?
I only laid my staff across the fingers
Of the pert varlet, when before my eyes,
By order of the governor, he tried
To drive away my handsome team of oxen.

FURST.
You are too rash by far. He did no more
Than what the governor had ordered him.

25

You had transgressed, and therefore should have paid
The penalty, however hard, in silence.

MELCHTHAL.
Was I to brook the fellow's saucy words?
"That if the peasant must have bread to eat;
Why, let him go and draw the plough himself!"
It cut me to the very soul to see
My oxen, noble creatures, when the knave
Unyoked them from the plough. As though they felt
The wrong, they lowed and butted with their horns.
On this I could contain myself no longer,
And, overcome by passion, struck him down.

FURST.
Oh, we old men can scarce command ourselves!
And can we wonder youth shall break its bounds?

MELCHTHAL.
I'm only sorry for my father's sake!
To be away from him, that needs so much
My fostering care! The governor detests him,
Because he hath, whene'er occasion served,
Stood stoutly up for right and liberty.
Therefore they'll bear him hard—the poor old man!
And there is none to shield him from their gripe.
Come what come may, I must go home again.

FURST.
Compose yourself, and wait in patience till
We get some tidings o'er from Unterwald.
Away! away! I hear a knock! Perhaps
A message from the viceroy! Get thee in!
You are not safe from Landenberger's <u>6</u> arm
In Uri, for these tyrants pull together.

MELCHTHAL.
They teach us Switzers what we ought to do.

FURST.
Away! I'll call you when the coast is clear.

[**MELCHTHAL** retires.

Unhappy youth! I dare not tell him all
The evil that my boding heart predicts!

Who's there? The door ne'er opens but I look
For tidings of mishap. Suspicion lurks
With darkling treachery in every nook.
Even to our inmost rooms they force their way,
These myrmidons of power; and soon we'll need
To fasten bolts and bars upon our doors.

[He opens the door and steps back in surprise as
WERNER STAUFFACHER enters.

What do I see? You, Werner? Now, by Heaven!
A valued guest, indeed. No man e'er set
His foot across this threshold more esteemed.
Welcome! thrice welcome, Werner, to my roof!
What brings you here? What seek you here in Uri?

STAUFFACHER (shakes FURST by the hand).
The olden times and olden Switzerland.

FURST.
You bring them with you. See how I'm rejoiced,
My heart leaps at the very sight of you.
Sit down—sit down, and tell me how you left
Your charming wife, fair Gertrude? Iberg's child,
And clever as her father. Not a man,
That wends from Germany, by Meinrad's Cell, 7
To Italy, but praises far and wide
Your house's hospitality. But say,
Have you come here direct from Flueelen,
And have you noticed nothing on your way,
Before you halted at my door?

STAUFFACHER (sits down).
        I saw
A work in progress, as I came along,
I little thought to see—that likes me ill.

FURST.
O friend! you've lighted on my thought at once.

STAUFFACHER.
Such things in Uri ne'er were known before.
Never was prison here in man's remembrance,
Nor ever any stronghold but the grave.

FURST.

27

You name it well. It is the grave of freedom.

STAUFFACHER.
Friend, Walter Furst, I will be plain with you.
No idle curiosity it is
That brings me here, but heavy cares. I left
Thraldom at home, and thraldom meets me here.
Our wrongs, e'en now, are more than we can bear.
And who shall tell us where they are to end?
From eldest time the Switzer has been free,
Accustomed only to the mildest rule.
Such things as now we suffer ne'er were known
Since herdsmen first drove cattle to the hills.

FURST.
Yes, our oppressions are unparalleled!
Why, even our own good lord of Attinghaus,
Who lived in olden times, himself declares
They are no longer to be tamely borne.

STAUFFACHER.
In Unterwalden yonder 'tis the same;
And bloody has the retribution been.
The imperial seneschal, the Wolfshot, who
At Rossberg dwelt, longed for forbidden fruits—
Baumgarten's wife, that lives at Alzellen,
He wished to overcome in shameful sort,
On which the husband slew him with his axe.

FURST.
Oh, Heaven is just in all its judgments still!
Baumgarten, say you? A most worthy man.
Has he escaped, and is he safely hid?

STAUFFACHER.
Your son-in-law conveyed him o'er the lake,
And he lies hidden in my house at Steinen.
He brought the tidings with him of a thing
That has been done at Sarnen, worse than all,
A thing to make the very heart run blood!

FURST (attentively).
Say on. What is it?

STAUFFACHER.
　　There dwells in Melchthal, then,

Just as you enter by the road from Kearns,
An upright man, named Henry of the Halden,
A man of weight and influence in the Diet.

FURST.
Who knows him not? But what of him? Proceed.

STAUFFACHER.
The Landenberg, to punish some offence,
Committed by the old man's son, it seems,
Had given command to take the youth's best pair
Of oxen from his plough: on which the lad
Struck down the messenger and took to flight.

FURST.
But the old father—tell me, what of him?

STAUFFACHER.
The Landenberg sent for him, and required
He should produce his son upon the spot;
And when the old man protested, and with truth,
That he knew nothing of the fugitive,
The tyrant called his torturers.

FURST (springs up and tries to lead him to the other side).
       Hush, no more!

STAUFFACHER (with increasing warmth).
"And though thy son," he cried, "Has escaped me now,
I have thee fast, and thou shalt feel my vengeance."
With that they flung the old man to the earth,
And plunged the pointed steel into his eyes.

FURST.
Merciful heavens!

MELCHTHAL (rushing out).
       Into his eyes, his eyes?

STAUFFACHER (addresses himself in astonishment to WALTER FURST).
Who is this youth?

MELCHTHAL (grasping him convulsively).
       Into his eyes? Speak, speak!

FURST.

Oh, miserable hour!

STAUFFACHER.
    Who is it, tell me?

[STAUFFACHER makes a sign to him.

It is his son! All righteous heaven!

MELCHTHAL.
        And I
Must be from thence! What! into both his eyes?

FURST.
Be calm, be calm; and bear it like a man!

MELCHTHAL.
And all for me—for my mad wilful folly!
Blind, did you say? Quite blind—and both his eyes?

STAUFFACHER.
Even so. The fountain of his sight's dried up.
He ne'er will see the blessed sunshine more.

FURST.
Oh, spare his anguish!

MELCHTHAL.
    Never, never more!

[Presses his hands upon his eyes and is silent for some
moments; then turning from one to the other, speaks in a
subdued tone, broken by sobs.

O the eye's light, of all the gifts of heaven,
The dearest, best! From light all beings live—
Each fair created thing—the very plants
Turn with a joyful transport to the light,
And he—he must drag on through all his days
In endless darkness! Never more for him
The sunny meads shall glow, the flowerets bloom;
Nor shall he more behold the roseate tints
Of the iced mountain top! To die is nothing,
But to have life, and not have sight—oh, that
Is misery indeed! Why do you look
So piteously at me? I have two eyes,

Yet to my poor blind father can give neither!
No, not one gleam of that great sea of light,
That with its dazzling splendor floods my gaze.

STAUFFACHER.

Ah, I must swell the measure of your grief,
Instead of soothing it. The worst, alas!
Remains to tell. They've stripped him of his all;
Naught have they left him, save his staff, on which,
Blind and in rags, he moves from door to door.

MELCHTHAL.

Naught but his staff to the old eyeless man!
Stripped of his all—even of the light of day,
The common blessing of the meanest wretch.
Tell me no more of patience, of concealment!
Oh, what a base and coward thing am I,
That on mine own security I thought
And took no care of thine! Thy precious head
Left as a pledge within the tyrant's grasp!
Hence, craven-hearted prudence, hence! And all
My thoughts be vengeance, and the despot's blood!
I'll seek him straight—no power shall stay me now—
And at his hands demand my father's eyes.
I'll beard him 'mid a thousand myrmidons!
What's life to me, if in his heart's best blood
I cool the fever of this mighty anguish.

[He is going.

FURST.

Stay, this is madness, Melchthal! What avails
Your single arm against his power? He sits
At Sarnen high within his lordly keep,
And, safe within its battlemented walls,
May laugh to scorn your unavailing rage.

MELCHTHAL.

And though he sat within the icy domes
Of yon far Schreckhorn—ay, or higher, where
Veiled since eternity, the Jungfrau soars,
Still to the tyrant would I make my way;
With twenty comrades minded like myself,
I'd lay his fastness level with the earth!
And if none follow me, and if you all,
In terror for your homesteads and your herds,

31

Bow in submission to the tyrant's yoke,
I'll call the herdsmen on the hills around me,
And there beneath heaven's free and boundless roof,
Where men still feel as men, and hearts are true
Proclaim aloud this foul enormity!

STAUFFACHER (to FURST).
'Tis at its height—and are we then to wait
Till some extremity——

MELCHTHAL.
          What extremity
Remains for apprehension, where men's eyes
Have ceased to be secure within their sockets?
Are we defenceless? Wherefore did we learn
To bend the crossbow—wield the battle-axe?
What living creature, but in its despair,
Finds for itself a weapon of defence?
The baited stag will turn, and with the show
Of his dread antlers hold the hounds at bay;
The chamois drags the huntsman down the abyss;
The very ox, the partner of man's toil,
The sharer of his roof, that meekly bends
The strength of his huge neck beneath the yoke,
Springs up, if he's provoked, whets his strong horn,
And tosses his tormenter to the clouds.

FURST.
If the three Cantons thought as we three do,
Something might, then, be done, with good effect.

STAUFFACHER.
When Uri calls, when Unterwald replies,
Schwytz will be mindful of her ancient league. 8

MELCHTHAL.
I've many friends in Unterwald, and none
That would not gladly venture life and limb
If fairly backed and aided by the rest.
Oh, sage and reverend fathers of this land,
Here do I stand before your riper years,
An unskilled youth whose voice must in the Diet
Still be subdued into respectful silence.
Do not, because that I am young and want
Experience, slight my counsel and my words.
'Tis not the wantonness of youthful blood

32

That fires my spirit; but a pang so deep
That even the flinty rocks must pity me.
You, too, are fathers, heads of families,
And you must wish to have a virtuous son
To reverence your gray hairs and shield your eyes
With pious and affectionate regard.
Do not, I pray, because in limb and fortune
You still are unassailed, and still your eyes
Revolve undimmed and sparkling in their spheres;
Oh, do not, therefore, disregard our wrongs!
Above you, too, doth hang the tyrant's sword.
You, too, have striven to alienate the land
From Austria. This was all my father's crime:
You share his guilt and may his punishment.

STAUFFACHER (to FURST).
Do then resolve! I am prepared to follow.

FURST.
First let us learn what steps the noble lords
Von Sillinen and Attinghaus propose.
Their names would rally thousands in the cause.

MELCHTHAL.
Is there a name within the Forest Mountains
That carries more respect than thine—and thine?
To names like these the people cling for help
With confidence—such names are household words.
Rich was your heritage of manly virtue,
And richly have you added to its stores.
What need of nobles? Let us do the work
Ourselves. Although we stood alone, methinks
We should be able to maintain our rights.

STAUFFACHER.
The nobles' wrongs are not so great as ours.
The torrent that lays waste the lower grounds
Hath not ascended to the uplands yet.
But let them see the country once in arms
They'll not refuse to lend a helping hand.

FURST.
Were there an umpire 'twixt ourselves and Austria,
Justice and law might then decide our quarrel.
But our oppressor is our emperor, too,
And judge supreme. 'Tis God must help us, then,

And our own arm! Be yours the task to rouse
The men of Schwytz; I'll rally friends in Uri.
But whom are we to send to Unterwald?

MELCHTHAL.
Thither send me. Whom should it more concern?

FURST.
No, Melchthal, no; thou art my guest, and I
Must answer for thy safety.

MELCHTHAL.
      Let me go.
I know each forest track and mountain pass;
Friends too I'll find, be sure, on every hand,
To give me willing shelter from the foe.

STAUFFACHER.
Nay, let him go; no traitors harbor there:
For tyranny is so abhorred in Unterwald
No minions can be found to work her will.
In the low valleys, too, the Alzeller
Will gain confederates and rouse the country.

MELCHTHAL.
But how shall we communicate, and not
Awaken the suspicion of the tyrants?

STAUFFACHER.
Might we not meet at Brunnen or at Treib,
Hard by the spot where merchant-vessels land?

FURST.
We must not go so openly to work.
Hear my opinion. On the lake's left bank,
As we sail hence to Brunnen, right against
The Mytenstein, deep-hidden in the wood
A meadow lies, by shepherds called the Rootli,
Because the wood has been uprooted there.
'Tis where our Canton boundaries verge on yours;—

   [To MELCHTHAL.

Your boat will carry you across from Schwytz.

   [To STAUFFACHER.

Thither by lonely by-paths let us wend
At midnight and deliberate o'er our plans.
Let each bring with him there ten trusty men,
All one at heart with us; and then we may
Consult together for the general weal,
And, with God's guidance, fix our onward course.

STAUFFACHER.
So let it be. And now your true right hand!
Yours, too, young man! and as we now three men
Among ourselves thus knit our hands together
In all sincerity and truth, e'en so
Shall we three Cantons, too, together stand
In victory and defeat, in life and death.

FURST and **MELCHTHAL.**
In life and death.

[They hold their hands clasped together for some moments in silence.

MELCHTHAL.
    Alas, my old blind father!
Thou canst no more behold the day of freedom;
But thou shalt hear it. When from Alp to Alp
The beacon-fires throw up their flaming signs,
And the proud castles of the tyrants fall,
Into thy cottage shall the Switzer burst,
Bear the glad tidings to thine ear, and o'er
Thy darkened way shall Freedom's radiance pour.

ACT II.

SCENE I.

The Mansion of the BARON OF ATTINGHAUSEN. A Gothic hall,
decorated with escutcheons and helmets. The BARON, a

gray-headed man, eighty-five years old, tall, and of a
commanding mien, clad in a furred pelisse, and leaning
on a staff tipped with chamois horn. KUONI and six hinds
standing round him, with rakes and scythes. ULRICH OF RUDENZ
enters in the costume of a knight.

RUDENZ.
Uncle, I'm here! Your will?

ATTINGHAUSEN.
      First let me share,
After the ancient custom of our house,
The morning-cup with these my faithful servants!

[He drinks from a cup, which is then passed round.

Time was I stood myself in field and wood,
With mine own eyes directing all their toil,
Even as my banner led them in the fight,
Now I am only fit to play the steward;
And, if the genial sun come not to me,
I can no longer seek it on the mountains.
Thus slowly, in an ever-narrowing sphere,
I move on to the narrowest and the last,
Where all life's pulses cease. I now am but
The shadow of my former self, and that
Is fading fast—'twill soon be but a name.

KUONI (offering RUDENZ the cup).
A pledge, young master!
   [RUDENZ hesitates to take the cup.
      Nay, sir, drink it off!
One cup, one heart! You know our proverb, sir!

ATTINGHAUSEN.
Go, children, and at eve, when work is done,
We'll meet and talk the country's business over.

[Exeunt Servants.

Belted and plumed, and all thy bravery on!
Thou art for Altdorf—for the castle, boy?

RUDENZ.
Yes, uncle. Longer may I not delay——

ATTINGHAUSEN (sitting down).
Why in such haste? Say, are thy youthful hours
Doled in such niggard measure that thou must
Be chary of then to thy aged uncle?

RUDENZ.
I see, my presence is not needed here,
I am but as a stranger in this house.

ATTINGHAUSEN (gazes fixedly at him for a considerable time).
Alas, thou art indeed! Alas, that home
To thee has grown so strange! Oh, Uly! Uly!
I scarce do know thee now, thus decked in silks,
The peacock's feather 9 flaunting in thy cap,
And purple mantle round thy shoulders flung;
Thou lookest upon the peasant with disdain,
And takest with a blush his honest greeting.

RUDENZ.
All honor due to him I gladly pay,
But must deny the right he would usurp.

ATTINGHAUSEN.
The sore displeasure of the king is resting
Upon the land, and every true man's heart
Is full of sadness for the grievous wrongs
We suffer from our tyrants. Thou alone
Art all unmoved amid the general grief.
Abandoning thy friends, thou takest thy stand
Beside thy country's foes, and, as in scorn
Of our distress, pursuest giddy joys,
Courting the smiles of princes, all the while
Thy country bleeds beneath their cruel scourge.

RUDENZ.
The land is sore oppressed; I know it, uncle.
But why? Who plunged it into this distress?
A word, one little easy word, might buy
Instant deliverance from such dire oppression,
And win the good-will of the emperor.
Woe unto those who seal the people's eyes,
And make them adverse to their country's good;
The men who, for their own vile, selfish ends,
Are seeking to prevent the Forest States
From swearing fealty to Austria's house,
As all the countries round about have done.

It fits their humor well, to take their seats
Amid the nobles on the Herrenbank;
They'll have the Caesar for their lord, forsooth,
That is to say, they'll have no lord at all.

ATTINGHAUSEN.
Must I hear this, and from thy lips, rash boy!

RUDENZ.
You urged me to this answer. Hear me out.
What, uncle, is the character you've stooped
To fill contentedly through life? Have you
No higher pride, than in these lonely wilds
To be the Landamman or Banneret,
The petty chieftain of a shepherd race?
How! Were it not a far more glorious choice
To bend in homage to our royal lord,
And swell the princely splendors of his court,
Than sit at home, the peer of your own vassals,
And share the judgment-seat with vulgar clowns?

ATTINGHAUSEN.
Ah, Uly, Uly; all too well I see,
The tempter's voice has caught thy willing ear,
And poured its subtle poison in thy heart.

RUDENZ.
Yes, I conceal it not. It doth offend
My inmost soul to hear the stranger's gibes,
That taunt us with the name of "Peasant Nobles."
Think you the heart that's stirring here can brook,
While all the young nobility around
Are reaping honor under Hapsburg's banner,
That I should loiter, in inglorious ease,
Here on the heritage my fathers left,
And, in the dull routine of vulgar toil,
Lose all life's glorious spring? In other lands
Deeds are achieved. A world of fair renown
Beyond these mountains stirs in martial pomp.
My helm and shield are rusting in the hall;
The martial trumpet's spirit-stirring blast,
The herald's call, inviting to the lists,
Rouse not the echoes of these vales, where naught
Save cowherd's horn and cattle-bell is heard,
In one unvarying, dull monotony.

ATTINGHAUSEN.

Deluded boy, seduced by empty show!
Despise the land that gave thee birth! Ashamed
Of the good ancient customs of thy sires!
The day will come, when thou, with burning tears,
Wilt long for home, and for thy native hills,
And that dear melody of tuneful herds,
Which now, in proud disgust, thou dost despise!
A day when thou wilt drink its tones in sadness,
Hearing their music in a foreign land.
Oh! potent is the spell that binds to home!
No, no, the cold, false world is not for thee.
At the proud court, with thy true heart thou wilt
Forever feel a stranger among strangers.
The world asks virtues of far other stamp
Than thou hast learned within these simple vales.
But go—go thither; barter thy free soul,
Take land in fief, become a prince's vassal,
Where thou might'st be lord paramount, and prince
Of all thine own unburdened heritage!
O, Uly, Uly, stay among thy people!
Go not to Altdorf. Oh, abandon not
The sacred cause of thy wronged native land!
I am the last of all my race. My name
Ends with me. Yonder hang my helm and shield;
They will be buried with me in the grave.
And must I think, when yielding up my breath,
That thou but wait'st the closing of mine eyes,
To stoop thy knee to this new feudal court,
And take in vassalage from Austria's hands
The noble lands, which I from God received
Free and unfettered as the mountain air!

RUDENZ.

'Tis vain for us to strive against the king.
The world pertains to him:—shall we alone,
In mad, presumptuous obstinacy strive
To break that mighty chain of lands, which he
Hath drawn around us with his giant grasp.
His are the markets, his the courts; his too
The highways; nay, the very carrier's horse,
That traffics on the Gotthardt, pays him toll.
By his dominions, as within a net,
We are enclosed, and girded round about.
—And will the empire shield us? Say, can it
Protect itself 'gainst Austria's growing power?

To God, and not to emperors, must we look!
What store can on their promises be placed,
When they, to meet their own necessities,
Can pawn, and even alienate the towns
That flee for shelter 'neath the eagle's wings?
No, uncle. It is wise and wholesome prudence,
In times like these, when faction's all abroad,
To own attachment to some mighty chief.
The imperial crown's transferred from line to line,
It has no memory for faithful service:
But to secure the favor of these great
Hereditary masters, were to sow
Seed for a future harvest.

ATTINGHAUSEN.
   Art so wise?
Wilt thou see clearer than thy noble sires,
Who battled for fair freedom's costly gem,
With life, and fortune, and heroic arm?
Sail down the lake to Lucerne, there inquire,
How Austria's rule doth weigh the Cantons down.
Soon she will come to count our sheep, our cattle,
To portion out the Alps, e'en to their summits,
And in our own free woods to hinder us
From striking down the eagle or the stag;
To set her tolls on every bridge and gate,
Impoverish us to swell her lust of sway,
And drain our dearest blood to feed her wars.
No, if our blood must flow, let it be shed
In our own cause! We purchase liberty
More cheaply far than bondage.

RUDENZ.
   What can we,
A shepherd race, against great Albert's hosts?

ATTINGHAUSEN.
Learn, foolish boy, to know this shepherd race!
I know them, I have led them on in fight—
I saw them in the battle at Favenz.
Austria will try, forsooth, to force on us
A yoke we are determined not to bear!
Oh, learn to feel from what a race thou'rt sprung!
Cast not, for tinsel trash and idle show,
The precious jewel of thy worth away.
To be the chieftain of a freeborn race,

Bound to thee only by their unbought love,
Ready to stand—to fight—to die with thee,
Be that thy pride, be that thy noblest boast!
Knit to thy heart the ties of kindred—home—
Cling to the land, the dear land of thy sires,
Grapple to that with thy whole heart and soul!
Thy power is rooted deep and strongly here,
But in yon stranger world thou'lt stand alone,
A trembling reed beat down by every blast.
Oh come! 'tis long since we have seen thee, Uly!
Tarry but this one day. Only to-day
Go not to Altdorf. Wilt thou? Not to-day!
For this one day bestow thee on thy friends.

[Takes his hand.

RUDENZ.
I gave my word. Unhand me! I am bound.

ATTINGHAUSEN (drops his hand and says sternly).
Bound, didst thou say? Oh yes, unhappy boy,
Thou art, indeed. But not by word or oath.
'Tis by the silken mesh of love thou'rt bound.

[**RUDENZ** turns away.

Ay, hide thee, as thou wilt. 'Tis she, I know,
Bertha of Bruneck, draws thee to the court;
'Tis she that chains thee to the emperor's service.
Thou think'st to win the noble, knightly maid,
By thy apostacy. Be not deceived.
She is held out before thee as a lure;
But never meant for innocence like thine.

RUDENZ.
No more; I've heard enough. So fare you well.

[Exit.

ATTINGHAUSEN.
Stay, Uly! Stay! Rash boy, he's gone! I can
Nor hold him back, nor save him from destruction.
And so the Wolfshot has deserted us;—
Others will follow his example soon.
This foreign witchery, sweeping o'er our hills,
Tears with its potent spell our youth away:

O luckless hour, when men and manners strange
Into these calm and happy valleys came,
To warp our primitive and guileless ways.
The new is pressing on with might. The old,
The good, the simple, fleeteth fast away.
New times come on. A race is springing up,
That think not as their fathers thought before!
What do I here? All, all are in the grave
With whom ere while I moved and held converse;
My age has long been laid beneath the sod:
Happy the man who may not live to see
What shall be done by those that follow me!

SCENE II.

A meadow surrounded by high rocks and wooded ground. On the
rocks are tracks, with rails and ladders, by which the peasants
are afterwards seen descending. In the background the lake is
observed, and over it a moon rainbow in the early part of the scene.
The prospect is closed by lofty mountains, with glaciers rising
behind them. The stage is dark, but the lake and glaciers glisten
in the moonlight.

MELCHTHAL, BAUMGARTEN, WINKELRIED, MEYER VON
SARNEN, BURKHART AM
BUHEL, ARNOLD VON SEWA, KLAUS VON DER FLUE, and four
other peasants,
all armed.

MELCHTHAL (behind the scenes).
The mountain pass is open. Follow me
I see the rock, and little cross upon it:
This is the spot; here is the Rootli.

[They enter with torches.

WINKELRIED.
          Hark!

SEWA.
The coast is clear.

MEYER.

None of our comrades come?
We are the first, we Unterwaldeners.

MELCHTHAL.

How far is't in the night?

BAUMGARTEN.

The beacon watch
Upon the Selisberg has just called two.

[A bell is heard at a distance.

MEYER.

Hush! Hark!

BUHEL.

The forest chapel's matin bell
Chimes clearly o'er the lake from Switzerland.

FLUE.

The air is clear, and bears the sound so far.

MELCHTHAL.

Go, you and you, and light some broken boughs,
Let's bid them welcome with a cheerful blaze.

[Two peasants exeunt.

SEWA.

The moon shines fair to-night. Beneath its beams
The lake reposes, bright as burnished steel.

BUHEL.

They'll have an easy passage.

WINKELRIED (pointing to the lake).

Ha! look there!
See you nothing?

MEYER.

What is it? Ay, indeed!
A rainbow in the middle of the night.

MELCHTHAL.

Formed by the bright reflection of the moon!

FLUE.
A sign most strange and wonderful, indeed!
Many there be who ne'er have seen the like.

SEWA.
'Tis doubled, see, a paler one above!

BAUMGARTEN.
A boat is gliding yonder right beneath it.

MELCHTHAL.
That must be Werner Stauffacher! I knew
The worthy patriot would not tarry long.

[Goes with BAUMGARTEN towards the shore.

MEYER.
The Uri men are like to be the last.

BUHEL.
They're forced to take a winding circuit through
The mountains; for the viceroy's spies are out.

[In the meanwhile the two peasants have kindled a fire
in the centre of the stage.

MELCHTHAL (on the shore).
Who's there? The word?

STAUFFACHER (from below).
      Friends of the country.

[All retire up the stage, towards the party landing from the boat.
Enter STAUFFACHER, ITEL, REDING, HANS AUF DER MAUER,
JORG IM HOPE,
    CONRAD HUNN, ULRICH DER SCHMIDT, JOST VON WEILER, and
three other
    peasants, armed.

ALL.
      Welcome!

[While the rest remain behind exchanging greetings, MELCHTHAL comes
forward with STAUFFACHER.

MELCHTHAL.

Oh, worthy Stauffacher, I've looked but now
On him, who could not look on me again.
I've laid my hands upon his rayless eyes,
And on their vacant orbits sworn a vow
Of vengeance, only to be cooled in blood.

STAUFFACHER.

Speak not of vengeance. We are here to meet
The threatened evil, not to avenge the past.
Now tell me what you've done, and what secured,
To aid the common cause in Unterwald.
How stands the peasantry disposed, and how
Yourself escaped the wiles of treachery?

MELCHTHAL.

Through the Surenen's fearful mountain chain,
Where dreary ice-fields stretch on every side,
And sound is none, save the hoarse vulture's cry,
I reached the Alpine pasture, where the herds
From Uri and from Engelberg resort,
And turn their cattle forth to graze in common.
Still as I went along, I slaked my thirst
With the coarse oozings of the lofty glacier,
That through the crevices come foaming down,
And turned to rest me in the herdsman's cots,
Where I was host and guest, until I gained
The cheerful homes and social haunts of men.
Already through these distant vales had spread
The rumor of this last atrocity;
And wheresoe'er I went, at every door,
Kind words and gentle looks were there to greet me.
I found these simple spirits all in arms
Against our rulers' tyrannous encroachments.
For as their Alps through each succeeding year
Yield the same roots,—their streams flow ever on
In the same channels,—nay, the clouds and winds
The selfsame course unalterably pursue,
So have old customs there, from sire to son,
Been handed down, unchanging and unchanged;
Nor will they brook to swerve or turn aside
From the fixed, even tenor of their life.
With grasp of their hard hands they welcomed me—
Took from the walls their rusty falchions down—
And from their eyes the soul of valor flashed
With joyful lustre, as I spoke those names,

Sacred to every peasant in the mountains,
Your own and Walter Fuerst's. Whate'er your voice
Should dictate as the right they swore to do;
And you they swore to follow e'en to death.
So sped I on from house to house, secure
In the guest's sacred privilege—and when
I reached at last the valley of my home,
Where dwell my kinsmen, scattered far and near—
And when I found my father stripped and blind,
Upon the stranger's straw, fed by the alms
Of charity——

STAUFFACHER.

    Great heaven!

MELCHTHAL.

        Yet wept I not!
No—not in weak and unavailing tears
Spent I the force of my fierce, burning anguish;
Deep in my bosom, like some precious treasure,
I locked it fast, and thought on deeds alone.
Through every winding of the hills I crept—
No valley so remote but I explored it;
Nay, even at the glacier's ice-clad base,
I sought and found the homes of living men;
And still, where'er my wandering footsteps turned,
The self-same hatred of these tyrants met me.
For even there, at vegetation's verge,
Where the numbed earth is barren of all fruits,
There grasping hands had been stretched forth for plunder.
Into the hearts of all this honest race,
The story of my wrongs struck deep, and now
They to a man are ours; both heart and hand.
Great things, indeed, you've wrought in little time.

MELCHTHAL.

I did still more than this. The fortresses,
Rossberg and Sarnen, are the country's dread;
For from behind their rocky walls the foe
Swoops, as the eagle from his eyrie, down,
And, safe himself, spreads havoc o'er the land.
With my own eyes I wished to weigh its strength,
So went to Sarnen, and explored the castle.

STAUFFACHER.

How! Risk thyself even in the tiger's den?

46

MELCHTHAL.
Disguised in pilgrim's weeds I entered it;
I saw the viceroy feasting at his board—
Judge if I'm master of myself or no!
I saw the tyrant, and I slew him not!

STAUFFACHER.
Fortune, indeed, has smiled upon your boldness.

[Meanwhile the others have arrived and join MELCHTHAL
and STAUFFACHER.

Yet tell me now, I pray, who are the friends,
The worthy men, who came along with you?
Make me acquainted with them, that we may
Speak frankly, man to man, and heart to heart.

MEYER.
In the three Cantons, who, sir, knows not you?
Meyer of Sarnen is my name; and this
Is Struth of Winkelried, my sister's son.

STAUFFACHER.
No unknown name. A Winkelried it was
Who slew the dragoon in the fen at Weiler,
And lost his life in the encounter, too.

WINKELRIED.
That, Master Stauffacher, was my grandfather.

MELCHTHAL (pointing to two peasants).
These two are men belonging to the convent
Of Engelberg, and live behind the forest.
You'll not think ill of them, because they're serfs,
And sit not free upon the soil, like us.
They love the land, and bear a good repute.

STAUFFACHER (to them).
Give me your hands. He has good cause for thanks,
That unto no man owes his body's service.
But worth is worth, no matter where 'tis found.

HUNN.
That is Herr Reding, sir, our old Landamman.

MEYER.

I know him well. There is a suit between us,
About a piece of ancient heritage.
Herr Reding, we are enemies in court,
Here we are one.

[Shakes his hand.

STAUFFACHER.

That's well and bravely said.

WINKELRIED.

Listen! They come. Hark to the horn of Uri!

[On the right and left armed men are seen descending
the rocks with torches.

MAUER.

Look, is not that God's pious servant there?
A worthy priest! The terrors of the night,
And the way's pains and perils scare not him,
A faithful shepherd caring for his flock.

BAUMGARTEN.

The Sacrist follows him, and Walter Fuerst.
But where is Tell? I do not see him there.

[WALTER FURST, ROSSELMANN the Pastor, PETERMANN the Sacrist,
KUONI the Shepherd, WERNI the huntsman, RUODI the Fisherman,
and five other countrymen, thirty-three in all, advance and
take their places round the fire.

FURST.

Thus must we, on the soil our fathers left us,
Creep forth by stealth to meet like murderers,
And in the night, that should their mantle lend
Only to crime and black conspiracy,
Assert our own good rights, which yet are clear
As is the radiance of the noonday sun.

MELCHTHAL.

So be it. What is woven in gloom of night
Shall free and boldly meet the morning light.

ROSSELMANN.

Confederates! listen to the words which God

Inspires my heart withal. Here we are met
To represent the general weal. In us
Are all the people of the land convened.
Then let us hold the Diet, as of old,
And as we're wont in peaceful times to do.
The time's necessity be our excuse
If there be aught informal in this meeting.
Still, wheresoe'er men strike for justice, there
Is God, and now beneath his heaven we stand.

STAUFFACHER.
'Tis well advised. Let us, then, hold the Diet
According to our ancient usages.
Though it be night there's sunshine in our cause.

MELCHTHAL.
Few though our numbers be, the hearts are here
Of the whole people; here the best are met.

HUNN.
The ancient books may not be near at hand,
Yet are they graven in our inmost hearts.

ROSSELMANN.
'Tis well. And now, then, let a ring be formed,
And plant the swords of power within the ground.

MAUER.
Let the Landamman step into his place,
And by his side his secretaries stand.

SACRIST.
There are three Cantons here. Which hath the right
To give the head to the united council?
Schwytz may contest the dignity with Uri,
We Unterwaldeners enter not the field.

MELCHTHAL.
We stand aside. We are not suppliants here,
Invoking aid from our more potent friends.

STAUFFACHER.
Let Uri have the sword. Her banner takes
In battle the precedence of our own.

FURST.

49

Schwytz, then, must share the honor of the sword;
For she's the honored ancestor of all.

ROSSELMANN.
Let me arrange this generous controversy.
Uri shall lead in battle—Schwytz in council.

FURST (gives STAUFFACHER his hand).
Then take your place.

STAUFFACHER.
        Not I. Some older man.

HOFE.
Ulrich, the smith, is the most aged here.

MAUER.
A worthy man, but he is not a freeman;
No bondman can be judge in Switzerland.

STAUFFACHER.
Is not Herr Reding here, our old Landamman?
Where can we find a worthier man than he?

FURST.
Let him be Amman and the Diet's chief?
You that agree with me hold up your hands!

[All hold up their right hands.

REDING (stepping into the centre).
I cannot lay my hands upon the books;
But by yon everlasting stars I swear
Never to swerve from justice and the right.

[The two swords are placed before him, and a circle formed;
Schwytz in the centre, Uri on his right, Unterwald on his left.

REDING (resting on his battle-sword).
Why, at the hour when spirits walk the earth,
Meet the three Cantons of the mountains here,
Upon the lake's inhospitable shore?
And what the purport of the new alliance
We here contract beneath the starry heaven?

STAUFFACHER (entering the circle).

50

No new alliance do we now contract,
But one our fathers framed, in ancient times,
We purpose to renew! For know, confederates,
Though mountain ridge and lake divide our bounds,
And every Canton's ruled by its own laws,
Yet are we but one race, born of one blood,
And all are children of one common home.

WINKELRIED.
Then is the burden of our legends true,
That we came hither from a distant land?
Oh, tell us what you know, that our new league
May reap fresh vigor from the leagues of old.

STAUFFACHER.
Hear, then, what aged herdsmen tell. There dwelt
A mighty people in the land that lies
Back to the north. The scourge of famine came;
And in this strait 'twas publicly resolved,
That each tenth man, on whom the lot might fall
Should leave the country. They obeyed—and forth,
With loud lamentings, men and women went,
A mighty host; and to the south moved on,
Cutting their way through Germany by the sword,
Until they gained that pine-clad hills of ours;
Nor stopped they ever on their forward course,
Till at the shaggy dell they halted, where
The Mueta flows through its luxuriant meads.
No trace of human creature met their eye,
Save one poor hut upon the desert shore,
Where dwelt a lonely man, and kept the ferry.
A tempest raged—the lake rose mountains high
And barred their further progress. Thereupon
They viewed the country; found it rich in wood,
Discovered goodly springs, and felt as they
Were in their own dear native land once more.
Then they resolved to settle on the spot;
Erected there the ancient town of Schwytz;
And many a day of toil had they to clear
The tangled brake and forest's spreading roots.
Meanwhile their numbers grew, the soil became
Unequal to sustain them, and they crossed
To the black mountain, far as Weissland, where,
Concealed behind eternal walls of ice,
Another people speak another tongue.
They built the village Stanz, beside the Kernwald

The village Altdorf, in the vale of Reuss;
Yet, ever mindful of their parent stem,
The men of Schwytz, from all the stranger race,
That since that time have settled in the land,
Each other recognize. Their hearts still know,
And beat fraternally to kindred blood.

[Extends his hand right and left.

MAUER.
Ay, we are all one heart, one blood, one race!

ALL (joining hands).
We are one people, and will act as one.

STAUFFACHER.
The nations round us bear a foreign yoke;
For they have yielded to the conqueror.
Nay, even within our frontiers may be found
Some that owe villein service to a lord,
A race of bonded serfs from sire to son.
But we, the genuine race of ancient Swiss,
Have kept our freedom from the first till now,
Never to princes have we bowed the knee;
Freely we sought protection of the empire.

ROSSELMANN.
Freely we sought it—freely it was given.
'Tis so set down in Emperor Frederick's charter.

STAUFFACHER.
For the most free have still some feudal lord.
There must be still a chief, a judge supreme,
To whom appeal may lie in case of strife.
And therefore was it that our sires allowed
For what they had recovered from the waste,
This honor to the emperor, the lord
Of all the German and Italian soil;
And, like the other freemen of his realm,
Engaged to aid him with their swords in war;
And this alone should be the freeman's duty,
To guard the empire that keeps guard for him.

MELCHTHAL.
He's but a slave that would acknowledge more.

STAUFFACHER.

They followed, when the Heribann went forth,
The imperial standard, and they fought its battles!
To Italy they marched in arms, to place
The Caesars' crown upon the emperor's head.
But still at home they ruled themselves in peace,
By their own laws and ancient usages.
The emperor's only right was to adjudge
The penalty of death; he therefore named
Some mighty noble as his delegate,
That had no stake or interest in the land.
He was called in, when doom was to be passed,
And, in the face of day, pronounced decree,
Clear and distinctly, fearing no man's hate.
What traces here, that we are bondsmen? Speak,
If there be any can gainsay my words!

HOFE.

No! You have spoken but the simple truth;
We never stooped beneath a tyrant's yoke.

STAUFFACHER.

Even to the emperor we refused obedience,
When he gave judgment in the church's favor;
For when the Abbey of Einsiedlen claimed
The Alp our fathers and ourselves had grazed,
And showed an ancient charter, which bestowed
The land on them as being ownerless—
For our existence there had been concealed—
What was our answer? This: "The grant is void,
No emperor can bestow what is our own:
And if the empire shall deny us justice,
We can, within our mountains, right ourselves!"
Thus spake our fathers! And shall we endure
The shame and infamy of this new yoke,
And from the vassal brook what never king
Dared in the fulness of his power attempt?
This soil we have created for ourselves,
By the hard labor of our hands; we've changed
The giant forest, that was erst the haunt
Of savage bears, into a home for man;
Extirpated the dragon's brood, that wont
To rise, distent with venom, from the swamps;
Rent the thick misty canopy that hung
Its blighting vapors on the dreary waste;
Blasted the solid rock; o'er the abyss

Thrown the firm bridge for the wayfaring man
By the possession of a thousand years
The soil is ours. And shall an alien lord,
Himself a vassal, dare to venture here,
On our own hearths insult us,—and attempt
To forge the chains of bondage for our hands,
And do us shame on our own proper soil?
Is there no help against such wrong as this?

   [Great sensation among the people.

Yes! there's a limit to the despot's power!
When the oppressed looks round in vain for justice,
When his sore burden may no more be borne,
With fearless heart he makes appeal to Heaven,
And thence brings down his everlasting rights,
Which there abide, inalienably his,
And indestructible as are the stars.
Nature's primeval state returns again,
Where man stands hostile to his fellow-man;
And if all other means shall fail his need,
One last resource remains—his own good sword.
Our dearest treasures call to us for aid
Against the oppressor's violence; we stand
For country, home, for wives, for children here!

ALL (clashing their swords).
Here stand we for our homes, our wives, and children.

ROSSELMANN (stepping into the circle).
Bethink ye well before ye draw the sword.
Some peaceful compromise may yet be made;
Speak but one word, and at your feet you'll see
The men who now oppress you. Take the terms
That have been often tendered you; renounce
The empire, and to Austria swear allegiance!

MAUER.
What says the priest? To Austria allegiance?

BUHEL.
Hearken not to him!

WINKELRLED.
    'Tis a traitor's counsel,
His country's foe!

54

REDING.
Peace, peace, confederates!

SEWA.
Homage to Austria, after wrongs like these!

FLUE.
Shall Austria exert from us by force
What we denied to kindness and entreaty?

MEYER.
Then should we all be slaves, deservedly.

MAUER.
Yes! Let him forfeit all a Switzer's rights
Who talks of yielding to the yoke of Austria!
I stand on this, Landamman. Let this be
The foremost of our laws!

MELCHTHAL.
Even so! Whoever
Shall talk of tamely bearing Austria's yoke,
Let him be stripped of all his rights and honors;
And no man hence receive him at his hearth!

ALL (raising their right hands).
Agreed! Be this the law!

REDING (after a pause).
The law it is.

ROSSELMANN.
Now you are free—by this law you are free.
Never shall Austria obtain by force
What she has failed to gain by friendly suit.

WEILER.
On with the order of the day! Proceed!

REDING.
Confederates! Have all gentler means been tried?
Perchance the emperor knows not of our wrongs,
It may not be his will that thus we suffer:
Were it not well to make one last attempt,
And lay our grievances before the throne,

55

Ere we unsheath the sword? Force is at best
A fearful thing even in a righteous cause;
God only helps when man can help no more.

STAUFFACHER (to CONRAD HUNN).
Here you can give us information. Speak!

HUNN.
I was at Rheinfeld, at the emperor's palace,
Deputed by the Cantons to complain
Of the oppression of these governors,
And claim the charter of our ancient freedom,
Which each new king till now has ratified.
I found the envoys there of many a town,
From Suabia and the valley of the Rhine,
Who all received their parchments as they wished
And straight went home again with merry heart.
They sent for me, your envoy, to the council,
Where I was soon dismissed with empty comfort;
"The emperor at present was engaged;
Some other time he would attend to us!"
I turned away, and passing through the hall,
With heavy heart in a recess I saw
The Grand Duke John in tears, and by his side
The noble lords of Wart and Tegerfeld,
Who beckoned me, and said, "Redress yourselves.
Expect not justice from the emperor.
Does he not plunder his own brother's child,
And keep from him his just inheritance?"
The duke claims his maternal property,
Urging he's now of age, and 'tis full time
That he should rule his people and dominions;
What is the answer made to him? The king
Places a chaplet on his head: "Behold,
The fitting ornament," he cries, "of youth!"

MAUER.
You hear. Expect not from the emperor
Or right, or justice. Then redress yourselves!

REDING.
No other course is left us. Now, advise
What plan most likely to insure success.

FURST.
To shake a thraldom off that we abhor,

To keep our ancient rights inviolate,
As we received them from our forefathers—this,
Not lawless innovation, is our aim.
Let Caesar still retain what is his due;
And he that is a vassal let him pay
The service he is sworn to faithfully.

MEYER.
I hold my land of Austria in fief.

FURST.
Continue, then, to pay your feudal service.

WEILER.
I'm tenant of the lords of Rappersweil.

FURST.
Continue, then, to pay them rent and tithe.

ROSSELMANN.
Of Zurich's lady, I'm the humble vassal.

FURST.
Give to the cloister what the cloister claims.

STAUFFACHER.
The empire only is my feudal lord.

FURST.
What needs must be, we'll do, but nothing further.
We'll drive these tyrants and their minions hence,
And raze their towering strongholds to the ground,
Yet shed, if possible, no drop of blood.
Let the emperor see that we were driven to cast
The sacred duties of respect away;
And when he finds we keep within our bounds,
His wrath, belike, may yield to policy;
For truly is that nation to be feared,
That, when in arms, is temperate in its wrath.

REDING.
But, prithee, tell us how may this be done?
The enemy is armed as well as we,
And, rest assured, he will not yield in peace.

STAUFFACHER.

He will, whene'er he sees us up in arms;
We shall surprise him, ere he is prepared.

MEYER.
'Tis easily said, but not so easily done.
Two fortresses of strength command the country.
They shield the foe, and should the king invade us,
The task would then be dangerous indeed.
Rossberg and Sarnen both must be secured,
Before a sword is drawn in either Canton.

STAUFFACHER.
Should we delay, the foe will soon be warned;
We are too numerous for secrecy.

MEYER.
There is no traitor in the Forest States.

ROSSELMANN.
But even zeal may heedlessly betray.

FURST.
Delay it longer, and the keep at Altdorf
Will be complete,—the governor secure.

MEYER.
You think but of yourselves.

SACRISTAN.
                    You are unjust!

MEYER.
Unjust! said you? Dares Uri taunt us so?

REDING.
Peace, on your oath!

MEYER.
            If Schwytz be leagued with Uri,
Why then, indeed, we must perforce be silent.

REDING.
And let me tell you, in the Diet's name,
Your hasty spirit much disturbs the peace.
Stand we not all for the same common cause?

WINKELRIED.
What, if we delay till Christmas? 'Tis then
The custom for the serfs to throng the castle,
Bringing the governor their annual gifts.
Thus may some ten or twelve selected men
Assemble unobserved within its walls,
Bearing about their persons pikes of steel,
Which may be quickly mounted upon staves,
For arms are not admitted to the fort.
The rest can fill the neighboring wood, prepared
To sally forth upon a trumpet's blast,
Whene'er their comrades have secured the gate;
And thus the castle will be ours with ease.

MELCHTHAL.
The Rossberg I will undertake to scale,
I have a sweetheart in the garrison,
Whom with some tender words I could persuade
To lower me at night a hempen ladder.
Once up, my friends will not be long behind.

REDING.
Are all resolved in favor of delay?

[The majority raise their hands.

STAUFFACHER (counting them).
Twenty to twelve is the majority.

FURST.
If on the appointed day the castles fall,
From mountain on to mountain we shall pass
The fiery signal: in the capital
Of every Canton quickly rouse the Landsturm.
Then, when these tyrants see our martial front,
Believe me, they will never make so bold
As risk the conflict, but will gladly take
Safe conduct forth beyond our boundaries.

STAUFFACHER.
Not so with Gessler. He will make a stand.
Surrounded with his dread array of horse,
Blood will he shed before he quits the field.
And even expelled he'd still be terrible.
'Tis hard, indeed 'tis dangerous, to spare him.

BAUMGARTEN.

Place me where'er a life is to be lost;
I owe my life to Tell, and cheerfully
Will pledge it for my country. I have cleared
My honor, and my heart is now at rest.

REDING.

Counsel will come with circumstance. Be patient.
Something must still be trusted to the moment.
Yet, while by night we hold our Diet here,
The morning, see, has on the mountain-tops
Kindled her glowing beacon. Let us part,
Ere the broad sun surprise us.

FURST.

   Do not fear.
The night wanes slowly from these vales of ours.

 [All have involuntarily taken off their caps, and
 contemplate the breaking of day, absorbed in silence.

ROSSELMANN.

By this fair light, which greeteth us, before
Those other nations, that, beneath us far,
In noisome cities pent, draw painful breath,
Swear we the oath of our confederacy!
We swear to be a nation of true brothers,
Never to part in danger or in death!

 [They repeat his words with three fingers raised.

We swear we will be free, as were our sires,
And sooner die than live in slavery!

 [All repeat as before.

We swear to put our trust in God Most High,
And not to quail before the might of man!

 [All repeat as before, and embrace each other.

STAUFFACHER.

Now every man pursue his several way
Back to his friends his kindred, and his home.
Let the herd winter up his flock and gain
In silence, friends, for our confederacy!

What for a time must be endured, endure.
And let the reckoning of the tyrants grow,
Till the great day arrive, when they shall pay
The general and particular debt at once.
Let every man control his own just rage,
And nurse his vengeance for the public wrongs;
For he whom selfish interest now engage
Defrauds the general weal of what to it belongs.

[As they are going off in profound silence, in three different
directions, the orchestra plays a solemn air. The empty scene
remains open for some time, showing the rays of the sun rising
over the glaciers.

ACT III.

SCENE I.

Court before TELL'S house. TELL with an axe. HEDWIG engaged
in her domestic duties. WALTER and WILHELM in the background
playing with a little cross-bow.

WALTER (sings).

With his cross-bow and his quiver
  The huntsman speeds his way,
Over mountain, dale, and river
  At the dawning of the day.

As the eagle, on wild pinion,
  Is the king in realms of air;
So the hunter claims dominion
  Over crag and forest lair.

Far as ever bow can carry
  Through the trackless, airy space,
All he sees he makes his quarry,

Soaring bird and beast of chase.

WILHELM (runs forward).
My string has snapped! Wilt mend it for me, father?

TELL.
Not I; a true-born archer helps himself.

[Boys retire.

HEDWIG.
The boys begin to use the bow betimes.

TELL.
'Tis early practice only makes the master.

HEDWIG.
Ah! Would to heaven they never learnt the art!

TELL.
But they shall learn it, wife, in all its points.
Whoe'er would carve an independent way
Through life must learn to ward or plant a blow.

HEDWIG.
Alas, alas! and they will never rest
Contentedly at home.

TELL.
            No more can I!
I was not framed by nature for a shepherd.
Restless I must pursue a changing course;
I only feel the flush and joy of life
In starting some fresh quarry every day.

HEDWIG.
Heedless the while of all your wife's alarms
As she sits watching through long hours at home.
For my soul sinks with terror at the tales
The servants tell about your wild adventures.
Whene'er we part my trembling heart forebodes
That you will ne'er come back to me again.
I see you on the frozen mountain steeps,
Missing, perchance, your leap from cliff to cliff;
I see the chamois, with a wild rebound,
Drag you down with him o'er the precipice.

I see the avalanche close o'er your head,
The treacherous ice give way, and you sink down
Entombed alive within its hideous gulf.
Ah! in a hundred varying forms does death
Pursue the Alpine huntsman on his course.
That way of life can surely ne'er be blessed,
Where life and limb are perilled every hour.

TELL.
The man that bears a quick and steady eye,
And trusts to God and his own lusty sinews,
Passes, with scarce a scar, through every danger.
The mountain cannot awe the mountain child.

[Having finished his work, he lays aside his tools.

And now, methinks, the door will hold awhile.
The axe at home oft saves the carpenter.

HEDWIG.
Whither away!

[Takes his cap.

TELL.
To Altdorf, to your father.

HEDWIG.
You have some dangerous enterprise in view? Confess!

TELL.
Why think you so?

HEDWIG.
    Some scheme's on foot,
Against the governors. There was a Diet
Held on the Rootli—that I know—and you
Are one of the confederacy I'm sure.

TELL.
I was not there. Yet will I not hold back
Whene'er my country calls me to her aid.

HEDWIG.
Wherever danger is, will you be placed.
On you, as ever, will the burden fall.

TELL.
Each man shall have the post that fits his powers.

HEDWIG.
You took—ay, 'mid the thickest of the storm—
The man of Unterwald across the lake.
'Tis a marvel you escaped. Had you no thought
Of wife and children then?

TELL.
   Dear wife, I had;
And therefore saved the father for his children.

HEDWIG.
To brave the lake in all its wrath; 'Twas not
To put your trust in God! 'Twas tempting him.

TELL.
The man that's over-cautious will do little.

HEDWIG.
Yes, you've a kind and helping hand for all;
But be in straits and who will lend you aid?

TELL.
God grant I ne'er may stand in need of it!

 [Takes up his crossbow and arrows.

HEDWIG.
Why take your crossbow with you? Leave it here.

TELL.
I want my right hand when I want my bow.

 [The boys return.

WALTER.
Where, father, are you going?

TELL.
   To grand-dad, boy—
To Altdorf. Will you go?

WALTER.

64

Ay, that I will!

HEDWIG.
The viceroy's there just now. Go not to Altdorf.

TELL.
He leaves to-day.

HEDWIG.
Then let him first be gone,
Cross not his path. You know he bears us grudge.

TELL.
His ill-will cannot greatly injure me.
I do what's right, and care for no man's hate.

HEDWIG.
'Tis those who do what's right whom he most hates.

TELL.
Because he cannot reach them. Me, I ween,
His knightship will be glad to leave in peace.

HEDWIG.
Ay! Are you sure of that?

TELL.
Not long ago,
As I was hunting through the wild ravines
Of Shechenthal, untrod by mortal foot,—
There, as I took my solitary way
Along a shelving ledge of rocks, where 'twas
Impossible to step on either side;
For high above rose, like a giant wall,
The precipice's side, and far below
The Shechen thundered o'er its rifted bed;—

[The boys press towards him, looking upon him
with excited curiosity.

There, face to face, I met the viceroy. He
Alone with me—and I myself alone—
Mere man to man, and near us the abyss.
And when his lordship had perused my face,
And knew the man he had severely fined
On some most trivial ground not long before;

And saw me, with my sturdy bow in hand,
Come striding towards him, then his cheek grew pale,
His knees refused their office, and I thought
He would have sunk against the mountain side.
Then, touched with pity for him, I advanced,
Respectfully, and said, "'Tis I, my lord."
But ne'er a sound could he compel his lips
To frame an answer. Only with his hand
He beckoned me in silence to proceed.
So I passed on, and sent his train to seek him.

HEDWIG.
He trembled then before you? Woe the while
You saw his weakness; that he'll not forgive.

TELL.
I shun him, therefore, and he'll not seek me.

HEDWIG.
But stay away to day. Go hunting rather!

TELL.
What do you fear?

HEDWIG.
    I am uneasy. Stay.

TELL.
Why thus distress yourself without a cause?

HEDWIG.
Because there is no cause. Tell, Tell! stay here!

TELL.
Dear wife, I gave my promise I would go.

HEDWIG.
Must you,—then go. But leave the boys with me.

WALTER.
No, mother dear, I'm going with my father.

HEDWIG.
How, Walter! Will you leave your mother then?

WALTER.

I'll bring you pretty things from grandpapa.

[Exit with his father.

WILHELM.
Mother, I'll stay with you!

HEDWIG (embracing him).
    Yes, yes! thou art
My own dear child. Thou'rt all that's left to me.

[She goes to the gate of the court, and looks anxiously
after TELL and her son for a considerable time.

SCENE II.

A retired part of the Forest. Brooks dashing in spray
over the rocks.

Enter BERTHA in a hunting dress. Immediately afterwards RUDENZ.

BERTHA.
He follows me. Now to explain myself!

RUDENZ (entering hastily).
At length, dear lady, we have met alone
In this wild dell, with rocks on every side,
No jealous eye can watch our interview.
Now let my heart throw off this weary silence.

BERTHA.
But are you sure they will not follow us?

RUDENZ.
See, yonder goes the chase. Now, then, or never!
I must avail me of the precious moment,—
Must hear my doom decided by thy lips,
Though it should part me from thy side forever.
Oh, do not arm that gentle face of thine
With looks so stern and harsh! Who—who am I,
That dare aspire so high as unto thee?
Fame hath not stamped me yet; nor may I take

67

My place amid the courtly throng of knights,
That, crowned with glory's lustre, woo thy smiles.
Nothing have I to offer but a heart
That overflows with truth and love for thee.

BERTHA (sternly and with severity).
And dare you speak to me of love—of truth?
You, that are faithless to your nearest ties!
You, that are Austria's slave—bartered and sold
To her—an alien, and your country's tyrant!

RUDENZ.
How! This reproach from thee! Whom do I seek
On Austria's side, my own beloved, but thee?

BERTHA.
Think you to find me in the traitor's ranks?
Now, as I live, I'd rather give my hand
To Gessler's self, all despot though he be,
Than to the Switzer who forgets his birth,
And stoops to be the minion of a tyrant.

RUDENZ.
Oh heaven, what must I hear!

BERTHA.
          Say! what can lie
Nearer the good man's heart than friends and kindred?
What dearer duty to a noble soul
Than to protect weak, suffering innocence,
And vindicate the rights of the oppressed?
My very soul bleeds for your countrymen;
I suffer with them, for I needs must love them;
They are so gentle, yet so full of power;
They draw my whole heart to them. Every day
I look upon them with increased esteem.
But you, whom nature and your knightly vow,
Have given them as their natural protector,
Yet who desert them and abet their foes,
In forging shackles for your native land,
You—you it is, that deeply grieve and wound me.
I must constrain my heart, or I shall hate you.

RUDENZ.
Is not my country's welfare all my wish?
What seek I for her but to purchase peace

'Neath Austria's potent sceptre?

BERTHA.
   Bondage, rather!
You would drive freedom from the last stronghold
That yet remains for her upon the earth.
The people know their own true interests better:
Their simple natures are not warped by show,
But round your head a tangling net is wound.

RUDENZ.
Bertha, you hate me—you despise me!

BERTHA.
Nay! And if I did, 'twere better for my peace.
But to see him despised and despicable,—
The man whom one might love.

RUDENZ.
   Oh, Bertha! You
Show me the pinnacle of heavenly bliss,
Then, in a moment, hurl me to despair!

BERTHA.
No, no! the noble is not all extinct
Within you. It but slumbers,—I will rouse it.
It must have cost you many a fiery struggle
To crush the virtues of your race within you.
But, heaven be praised, 'tis mightier than yourself,
And you are noble in your own despite!

RUDENZ.
You trust me, then? Oh, Bertha, with thy love
What might I not become?

BERTHA.
   Be only that
For which your own high nature destined you.
Fill the position you were born to fill;—
Stand by your people and your native land.
And battle for your sacred rights!

RUDENZ.
Alas! How can I hope to win you—to possess you,
If I take arms against the emperor?
Will not your potent kinsman interpose,

To dictate the disposal of your hand?

BERTHA.
All my estates lie in the Forest Cantons;
And I am free, when Switzerland is free.

RUDENZ.
Oh! what a prospect, Bertha, hast thou shown me!

BERTHA.
Hope not to win my hand by Austria's favor;
Fain would they lay their grasp on my estates,
To swell the vast domains which now they hold.
The selfsame lust of conquest that would rob
You of your liberty endangers mine.
Oh, friend, I'm marked for sacrifice;—to be
The guerdon of some parasite, perchance!
They'll drag me hence to the imperial court
That hateful haunt of falsehood and intrigue;
There do detested marriage bonds await me.
Love, love alone,—your love can rescue me.

RUDENZ.
And thou could'st be content, love, to live here,
In my own native land to be my own?
Oh, Bertha, all the yearnings of my soul
For this great world and its tumultuous strife,
What were they, but a yearning after thee?
In glory's path I sought for thee alone
And all my thirst of fame was only love.
But if in this calm vale thou canst abide
With me, and bid earth's pomps and pride adieu,
Then is the goal of my ambition won;
And the rough tide of the tempestuous world
May dash and rave around these firm-set hills!
No wandering wishes more have I to send
Forth to the busy scene that stirs beyond.
Then may these rocks that girdle us extend
Their giants walls impenetrably round,
And this sequestered happy vale alone
Look up to heaven, and be my paradise!

BERTHA.
Now art thou all my fancy dreamed of thee.
My trust has not been given to thee in vain.

RUDENZ.

Away, ye idle phantoms of my folly!
In mine own home I'll find my happiness.
Here where the gladsome boy to manhood grew,
Where every brook, and tree, and mountain peak,
Teems with remembrances of happy hours,
In mine own native land thou wilt be mine.
Ah, I have ever loved it well, I feel
How poor without it were all earthly joys.

BERTHA.

Where should we look for happiness on earth,
If not in this dear land of innocence?
Here, where old truth hath its familiar home,
Where fraud and guile are strangers, envy ne'er
Shall dim the sparkling fountain of our bliss,
And ever bright the hours shall o'er us glide.
There do I see thee, in true manly worth,
The foremost of the free and of thy peers,
Revered with homage pure and unconstrained,
Wielding a power that kings might envy thee.

RUDENZ.

And thee I see, thy sex's crowning gem,
With thy sweet woman grace and wakeful love,
Building a heaven for me within my home,
And, as the springtime scatters forth her flowers,
Adorning with thy charms my path of life,
And spreading joy and sunshine all around.

BERTHA.

And this it was, dear friend, that caused my grief,
To see thee blast this life's supremest bliss,
With thine own hand. Ah! what had been my fate,
Had I been forced to follow some proud lord,
Some ruthless despot, to his gloomy castle!
Here are no castles, here no bastioned walls
Divide me from a people I can bless.

RUDENZ.

Yet, how to free myself; to loose the coils
Which I have madly twined around my head?

BERTHA.

Tear them asunder with a man's resolve.
Whatever the event, stand by the people.

It is thy post by birth.

[Hunting horns are heard in the distance.

But hark! The chase!
Farewell,—'tis needful we should part—away!
Fight for thy land; thou lightest for thy love.
One foe fills all our souls with dread; the blow
That makes one free emancipates us all.

[Exeunt severally.

SCENE III.

A meadow near Altdorf. Trees in the foreground. At the back
of the stage a cap upon a pole. The prospect is bounded by
the Bannberg, which is surmounted by a snow-capped mountain.

FRIESSHARDT and LEUTHOLD on guard.

FRIESSHARDT.
We keep our watch in vain. There's not a soul
Will pass and do obeisance to the cap.
But yesterday the place swarmed like a fair;
Now the whole green looks like a very desert,
Since yonder scarecrow hung upon the pole.

LEUTHHOLD.
Only the vilest rabble show themselves,
And wave their tattered caps in mockery at us.
All honest citizens would sooner make
A tedious circuit over half the town
Than bend their backs before our master's cap.

FRIESSHARDT.
They were obliged to pass this way at noon,
As they were coming from the council house.
I counted then upon a famous catch,
For no one thought of bowing to the cap.
But Rosselmann, the priest, was even with me:
Coming just then from some sick penitent,
He stands before the pole—raises the Host—

The Sacrist, too, must tinkle with his bell—
When down they dropped on knee—myself and all
In reverence to the Host, but not the cap.

LEUTHOLD.

Hark ye, companion, I've a shrewd suspicion,
Our post's no better than the pillory.
It is a burning shame, a trooper should
Stand sentinel before an empty cap,
And every honest fellow must despise us,
To do obeisance to a cap, too! Faith,
I never heard an order so absurd!

FRIESSHARDT.

Why not, an't please thee, to an empty cap.
Thou'st ducked, I'm sure, to many an empty sconce.

[HILDEGARD, MECHTHILD, and ELSBETH enter with their children
and station themselves around the pole.

LEUTHOLD.

And thou art an officious sneaking knave,
That's fond of bringing honest folks to trouble.
For my part, he that likes may pass the cap
I'll shut my eyes and take no note of him.

MECHTHILD.

There hangs the viceroy! Your obeisance, children!

ELSBETH.

I would to God he'd go, and leave his cap!
The country would be none the worse for it.

FRIESSHARDT (driving them away).

Out of the way! Confounded pack of gossips!
Who sent for you? Go, send your husbands here,
If they have courage to defy the order.

[TELL enters with his crossbow, leading his son WALTER
by the hand. They pass the hat without noticing it, and
advance to the front of the stage.

WALTER (pointing to the Bannberg).

Father, is't true, that on the mountain there,
The trees, if wounded with a hatchet, bleed?

73

TELL.
Who says so, boy?

WALTER.
 The master herdsman, father!
He tells us there's a charm upon the trees,
And if a man shall injure them, the hand
That struck the blow will grow from out the grave.

TELL.
There is a charm about them, that's the truth.
Dost see those glaciers yonder, those white horns,
That seem to melt away into the sky?

WALTER.
They are the peaks that thunder so at night,
And send the avalanches down upon us.

TELL.
They are; and Altdorf long ago had been
Submerged beneath these avalanches' weight,
Did not the forest there above the town
Stand like a bulwark to arrest their fall.

WALTER (after musing a little).
And are there countries with no mountains, father?

TELL.
Yes, if we travel downwards from our heights,
And keep descending in the rivers' courses,
We reach a wide and level country, where
Our mountain torrents brawl and foam no more,
And fair, large rivers glide serenely on.
All quarters of the heaven may there be scanned
Without impediment. The corn grows there
In broad and lovely fields, and all the land
Is fair as any garden to the view.

WALTER.
But, father, tell me, wherefore haste we not
Away to this delightful land, instead
Of toiling here, and struggling as we do?

TELL.
The land is fair and bountiful as Heaven;
But they who till it never may enjoy

74

The fruits of what they sow.

WALTER.
>   Live they not free,
As you do, on the land their fathers left them?

TELL.
The fields are all the bishop's or the king's.

WALTER.
But they may freely hunt among the woods?

TELL.
The game is all the monarch's—bird and beast.

WALTER.
But they, at least, may surely fish the streams?

TELL.
Stream, lake, and sea, all to the king belong.

WALTER.
Who is this king, of whom they're so afraid?

TELL.
He is the man who fosters and protects them.

WALTER.
Have they not courage to protect themselves?

TELL.
The neighbor there dare not his neighbor trust.

WALTER.
I should want breathing room in such a land,
I'd rather dwell beneath the avalanches.

TELL.
'Tis better, child, to have these glacier peaks
Behind one's back than evil-minded men!

[They are about to pass on.

WALTER.
See, father, see the cap on yonder pole!

75

TELL.
What is the cap to us? Come, let's be gone.

[As he is going, FRIESSHARDT, presenting his pike, stops him.

FRIESSHARDT.
Stand, I command you, in the emperor's name.

TELL (seizing the pike).
What would ye? Wherefore do ye stop my path?

FRIESSHARDT.
You've broke the mandate, and must go with us.

LEUTHOLD.
You have not done obeisance to the cap.

TELL.
Friend, let me go.

FRIESSHARDT.
 Away, away to prison!

WALTER.
Father to prison! Help!
 [Calling to the side scene.
  This way, you men!
Good people, help! They're dragging him to prison!

[ROSSELMANN, the priest, and the SACRISTAN, with
three other men, enter.

SACRISTAN.
What's here amiss?

ROSSELMANN.
 Why do you seize this man?

FRIESSHARDT.
He is an enemy of the king—a traitor!

TELL (seizing him with violence).
A traitor, I!

ROSSELMANN.
 Friend, thou art wrong. 'Tis Tell,

An honest man, and worthy citizen.

WALTER (descries FURST, and runs up to him).
Grandfather, help! they want to seize my father!

FRIESSHARDT.
Away to prison!

FURST (running in).
    Stay! I offer bail.
For God's sake, Tell, what is the matter here?

    [MELCHTHAL and STAUFFACHER enter.

LEUTHOLD.
He has contemned the viceroy's sovereign power,
Refusing flatly to acknowledge it.

STAUFFACHER.
Has Tell done this?

MELCHTHAL.
    Villain, thou knowest 'tis false!

LEUTHOLD.
He has not made obeisance to the cap.

FURST.
And shall for this to prison? Come, my friend,
Take my security, and let him go.

FRIESSHARDT.
Keep your security for yourself—you'll need it.
We only do our duty. Hence with him.

MELCHTHAL (to the country people).
This is too bad—shall we stand by, and see them.
Drag him away before our very eyes?

SACRISTAN.
We are the strongest. Don't endure it, friends.
Our countrymen will back us to a man.

FRIESSHARDT.
Who dares resist the governor's commands?

OTHER THREE PEASANTS (running in).
We'll help you. What's the matter? Down with them!

[HILDEGARD, MECHTHILD, and ELSBETH return.

TELL.
Go, go, good people, I can help myself.
Think you, had I a mind to use my strength,
These pikes of theirs should daunt me?

MELCHTHAL (to FRIESSHARDT).
      Only try—
Try, if you dare, to force him from amongst us.

FURST and **STAUFFACHER.**
Peace, peace, friends!

FRIESSHARDT (loudly).
     Riot! Insurrection, ho!

[Hunting horns without.

WOMEN.
The governor!

FRIESSHARDT (raising his voice).
     Rebellion! Mutiny!

STAUFFACHER.
Roar, till you burst, knave!

ROSSELMANN and **MELCHTHAL.**
     Will you hold your tongue?

FRIESSHARDT (calling still louder).
Help, help, I say, the servants of the law!

FURST.
The viceroy here! Then we shall smart for this!

[Enter GESSLER on horseback, with a falcon on his wrist;
RUDOLPH DER HARRAS, BERTHA, and RUDENZ, and a numerous
train of armed attendants, who form a circle of lances
around the whole stage.

HARRAS.

Room for the viceroy!

GESSLER.
          Drive the clowns apart.
Why throng the people thus? Who calls for help?

[General silence.

Who was it? I will know.

[**FRIESSHARDT** steps forward.

          And who art thou?
And why hast thou this man in custody?

[Gives his falcon to an attendant.

FRIESSHARDT.
Dread sir, I am a soldier of your guard,
And stationed sentinel beside the cap;
This man I apprehended in the act
Of passing it without obeisance due,
So I arrested him, as you gave order,
Whereon the people tried to rescue him.

GESSLER (after a pause).
And do you, Tell, so lightly hold your king,
And me, who act as his vicegerent here,
That you refuse the greeting to the cap
I hung aloft to test your loyalty?
I read in this a disaffected spirit.

TELL.
Pardon me, good my lord! The action sprung
From inadvertence,—not from disrespect.
Were I discreet, I were not William Tell.
Forgive me now—I'll not offend again.

GESSLER (after a pause).
I hear, Tell, you're a master with the bow,—
And bear the palm away from every rival.

WALTER.
That must be true, sir! At a hundred yards
He'll shoot an apple for you off the tree.

GESSLER.

Is that boy thine, Tell?

TELL.

  Yes, my gracious lord.

GESSLER.

Hast any more of them?

TELL.

  Two boys, my lord.

GESSLER.

And, of the two, which dost thou love the most?

TELL.

Sir, both the boys are dear to me alike.

GESSLER.

Then, Tell, since at a hundred yards thou canst
Bring down the apple from the tree, thou shalt
Approve thy skill before me. Take thy bow—
Thou hast it there at hand—and make thee ready
To shoot an apple from the stripling's head!
But take this counsel,—look well to thine aim,
See that thou hittest the apple at the first,
For, shouldst thou miss, thy head shall pay the forfeit.

 [All give signs of horror.

TELL.

What monstrous thing, my lord, is this you ask?
That I, from the head of mine own child!—No, no!
It cannot be, kind sir, you meant not that—
God in His grace forbid! You could not ask
A father seriously to do that thing!

GESSLER.

Thou art to shoot an apple from his head!
I do desire—command it so.

TELL.

  What, I!
Level my crossbow at the darling head
Of mine own child? No—rather let me die!

GESSLER.
Or thou must shoot, or with thee dies the boy.

TELL.
Shall I become the murderer of my child!
You have no children, sir—you do not know
The tender throbbings of a father's heart.

GESSLER.
How now, Tell, so discreet upon a sudden
I had been told thou wert a visionary,—
A wanderer from the paths of common men.
Thou lovest the marvellous. So have I now
Culled out for thee a task of special daring.
Another man might pause and hesitate;
Thou dashest at it, heart and soul, at once.

BERTHA.
Oh, do not jest, my lord, with these poor souls!
See, how they tremble, and how pale they look,
So little used are they to hear thee jest.

GESSLER.
Who tells thee that I jest?

[Grasping a branch above his head.

Here is the apple.
Room there, I say! And let him take his distance—
Just eighty paces-as the custom is
Not an inch more or less! It was his boast,
That at a hundred he could hit his man.
Now, archer, to your task, and look you miss not!

HARRAS:
Heavens! this grows serious—down, boy, on your knees,
And beg the governor to spare your life.

FURST (aside to MELCHTHAL, who can scarcely restrain his impatience).
Command yourself—be calm, I beg of you!

BERTHA (to the governor).
Let this suffice you, sir! It is inhuman
To trifle with a father's anguish thus.
Although this wretched man had forfeited
Both life and limb for such a slight offence,

Already has he suffered tenfold death.
Send him away uninjured to his home;
He'll know thee well in future; and this hour
He and his children's children will remember.

GESSLER.
Open a way there—quick! Why this delay?
Thy life is forfeited; I might despatch thee,
And see I graciously repose thy fate
Upon the skill of thine own practised hand.
No cause has he to say his doom is harsh,
Who's made the master of his destiny.
Thou boastest of thy steady eye. 'Tis well!
Now is a fitting time to show thy skill.
The mark is worthy, and the prize is great.
To hit the bull's-eye in the target; that
Can many another do as well as thou;
But he, methinks, is master of his craft
Who can at all times on his skill rely,
Nor lets his heart disturb or eye or hand.

FURST.
My lord, we bow to your authority;
But, oh, let justice yield to mercy here.
Take half my property, nay, take it all,
But spare a father this unnatural doom!

WALTER.
Grandfather, do not kneel to that bad man!
Say, where am I to stand? I do not fear;
My father strikes the bird upon the wing,
And will not miss now when 'twould harm his boy!

STAUFFACHER.
Does the child's innocence not touch your heart?

ROSSELMANN.
Bethink you, sir, there is a God in heaven,
To whom you must account for all your deeds.

GESSLER (pointing to the boy).
Bind him to yonder lime tree straight!

WALTER.
Bind me? No, I will not be bound! I will be still,
Still as a lamb—nor even draw my breath!

But if you bind me I cannot be still.
Then I shall writhe and struggle with my bonds.

HARRAS.
But let your eyes at least be bandaged, boy!

WALTER.
And why my eyes? No! Do you think I fear
An arrow from my father's hand? Not I!
I'll wait it firmly, nor so much as wink!
Quick, father, show them that thou art an archer!
He doubts thy skill—he thinks to ruin us.
Shoot then and hit though but to spite the tyrant!

[He goes to the lime tree, and an apple is placed on his head.

MELCHTHAL (to the country people).
What! Is this outrage to be perpetrated
Before our very eyes? Where is our oath?

STAUFFACHER.
'Tis all in vain. We have no weapons here;
And see the wood of lances that surrounds us!

MELCHTHAL.
Oh! would to heaven that we had struck at once!
God pardon those who counselled the delay!

GESSLER (to TELL).
Now, to thy task! Men bear not arms for naught.
'Tis dangerous to carry deadly weapons,
And on the archer oft his shaft recoils.
This right these haughty peasant-churls assume
Trenches upon their master's privileges.
None should be armed but those who bear command.
It pleases you wear the bow and bolt;
Well, be it so. I will provide the mark.

TELL (bends the bow and fixes the arrow).
A lane there! Room!

STAUFFACHER.
What, Tell? You would—no, no!
You shake—your hand's unsteady—your knees tremble!

TELL (letting the bow sink down).

83

There's something swims before mine eyes!

WOMEN.
Great Heaven!

TELL.
> Release me from this shot!
Here is my heart!

[Tears open his breast.

Summon your troopers—let them strike me down!

GESSLER.
I do not want thy life, Tell, but the shot.
Thy talent's universal! Nothing daunts thee!
Thou canst direct the rudder like the bow!
Storms fright not thee when there's a life at stake.
Now, savior, help thyself, thou savest all!

[TELL stands fearfully agitated by contending emotions,
his hands moving convulsively, and his eyes turning
alternately to the governor and heaven. Suddenly he
takes a second arrow from his quiver and sticks it in
his belt. The governor watches all these motions.

WALTER (beneath the lime tree).
Come, father, shoot! I'm not afraid!

TELL.
> It must be!

[Collects himself and levels the bow.

RUDENZ (who all the while has been standing in a state of violent
excitement, and has with difficulty restrained himself, advances).
My lord, you will not urge this matter further.
You will not. It was surely but a test.
You've gained your object. Rigor pushed too far
Is sure to miss its aim, however good,

As snaps the bow that's all too straightly bent.

GESSLER.
Peace, till your counsel's asked for!

RUDENZ.
I will speak! Ay, and I dare! I reverence my king;
But acts like these must make his name abhorred.
He sanctions not this cruelty. I dare
Avouch the fact. And you outstep your powers
In handling thus an unoffending people.

GESSLER.
Ha! thou growest bold methinks!

RUDENZ.
      I have been dumb
To all the oppressions I was doomed to see.
I've closed mine eyes that they might not behold them,
Bade my rebellious, swelling heart be still,
And pent its struggles down within my breast.
But to be silent longer were to be
A traitor to my king and country both.

BERTHA (casting herself between him and the governor).
Oh, heavens! you but exasperate his rage!

RUDENZ.
My people I forsook, renounced my kindred—
Broke all the ties of nature that I might
Attach myself to you. I madly thought
That I should best advance the general weal,
By adding sinews to the emperor's power.
The scales have fallen from mine eyes—I see
The fearful precipice on which I stand.
You've led my youthful judgment far astray,—
Deceived my honest heart. With best intent,
I had well nigh achieved my country's ruin.

GESSLER.
Audacious boy, this language to thy lord?

RUDENZ.
The emperor is my lord, not you! I'm free
As you by birth, and I can cope with you
In every virtue that beseems a knight.

And if you stood not here in that king's name,
Which I respect e'en where 'tis most abused,
I'd throw my gauntlet down, and you should give
An answer to my gage in knightly fashion.
Ay, beckon to your troopers! Here I stand;
But not like these—
    [Pointing to the people.
            unarmed. I have a sword,
And he that stirs one step——

STAUFFACHER (exclaims).
    The apple's down!

[While the attention of the crowd has been directed
to the spot where BERTHA had cast herself between RUDENZ
and GESSLER, TELL has shot.

ROSSELMANN.
The boy's alive!

MANY VOICES.
    The apple has been struck!

[**WALTER FURST** staggers, and is about to fall. BERTHA supports him.

GESSLER (astonished).
How? Has he shot? The madman!

BERTHA.
        Worthy father!
Pray you compose yourself. The boy's alive!

WALTER (runs in with the apple).
Here is the apple, father! Well I knew
You would not harm your boy.

[TELL stands with his body bent forwards, as though he would
follow the arrow. His bow drops from his hand. When he sees
the boy advancing, he hastens to meet him with open arms, and
embracing him passionately sinks down with him quite exhausted.
All crowd round them deeply affected.

BERTHA.
Oh, ye kind heavens!

FURST (to father and son).

My children, my dear children!

STAUFFACHER.
God be praised!

LEUTHOLD.
        Almighty powers! That was a shot indeed!
It will be talked of to the end of time.

HARRAS.
This feat of Tell, the archer, will be told
While yonder mountains stand upon their base.

    [Hands the apple to GESSLER.

GESSLER.
By heaven! the apple's cleft right through the core.
It was a master shot I must allow.

ROSSELMANN.
The shot was good. But woe to him who drove
The man to tempt his God by such a feat!

STAUFFACHER.
Cheer up, Tell, rise! You've nobly freed yourself,
And now may go in quiet to your home.

ROSSELMANN.
Come, to the mother let us bear her son!

GESSLER.
A word, Tell.

    [They are about to lead him off.

TELL.
    Sir, your pleasure?

GESSLER.
        Thou didst place
A second arrow in thy belt—nay, nay!
I saw it well—what was thy purpose with it?

TELL (confused).
It is the custom with all archers, sir.

GESSLER.
No, Tell, I cannot let that answer pass.
There was some other motive, well I know.
Frankly and cheerfully confess the truth;—
Whate'er it be I promise thee thy life,
Wherefore the second arrow?

TELL.
             Well, my lord,
Since you have promised not to take my life,
I will, without reserve, declare the truth.

   [He draws the arrow from his belt, and fixes his eyes
   sternly upon the governor.

If that my hand had struck my darling child,
This second arrow I had aimed at you,
And, be assured, I should not then have missed.

GESSLER.
Well, Tell, I promised thou shouldst have thy life;
I gave my knightly word, and I will keep it.
Yet, as I know the malice of thy thoughts,
I will remove thee hence to sure confinement,
Where neither sun nor moon shall reach thine eyes,
Thus from thy arrows I shall be secure.
Seize on him, guards, and bind him.

   [They bind him.

STAUFFACHER.
             How, my lord—
How can you treat in such a way a man
On whom God's hand has plainly been revealed?

GESSLER.
Well, let us see if it will save him twice!
Remove him to my ship; I'll follow straight.
In person I will see him lodged at Kuessnacht.

ROSSELMANN.
You dare not do it. Nor durst the emperor's self,
So violate our dearest chartered rights.

GESSLER.
Where are they? Has the emperor confirmed them?

He never has. And only by obedience
Need you expect to win that favor from him.
You are all rebels 'gainst the emperor's power
And bear a desperate and rebellious spirit.
I know you all—I see you through and through.
Him do I single from amongst you now,
But in his guilt you all participate.
The wise will study silence and obedience.

[Exit, followed by BERTHA, RUDENZ, HARRAS, and attendants.
FRIESSHARDT and LEUTHOLD remain.

FURST (in violent anguish).
All's over now! He is resolved to bring
Destruction on myself and all my house.

STAUFFACHER (to Tell).
Oh, why did you provoke the tyrant's rage?

TELL.
Let him be calm who feels the pangs I felt.

STAUFFACHER.
Alas! alas! Our every hope is gone.
With you we all are fettered and enchained.

COUNTRY PEOPLE (surrounding Tell).
Our last remaining comfort goes with you!

LEUTHOLD (approaching him).
I'm sorry for you, Tell, but must obey.

TELL.
Farewell!

WALTER (clinging to him in great agony).
    Oh, father, father, father dear!

TELL (pointing to Heaven).
Thy father is on high—appeal to Him!

STAUFFACHER.
Hast thou no message, Tell, to send your wife?

TELL (clasping the boy passionately to his breast).
The boy's uninjured; God will succor me!

[Tears himself suddenly away, and follows the soldiers of the guard.

SCENE I.

Eastern shore of the Lake of Lucerne; rugged and singularly shaped rocks close the prospect to the west. The lake is agitated, violent roaring and rushing of wind, with thunder and lightning at intervals.

KUNZ OF GERSAU, FISHERMAN and **BOY.**
KUNZ.
I saw it with these eyes! Believe me, friend,
It happen'd all precisely as I've said.

FISHERMAN.
Tell, made a prisoner, and borne off to Kuessnacht?
The best man in the land, the bravest arm,
Had we resolved to strike for liberty!

KUNZ.
The Viceroy takes him up the lake in person:
They were about to go on board, as I
Left Flueelen; but still the gathering storm,
That drove me here to land so suddenly,
Perchance has hindered their abrupt departure.

FISHERMAN.
Our Tell in chains, and in the viceroy's power!
Oh, trust me, Gessler will entomb him where
He never more shall see the light of day;
For, Tell once free, the tyrant well may dread
The just revenge of one so deep incensed.

90

KUNZ.

The old Landamman, too—von Attinghaus—
They say, is lying at the point of death.

FISHERMAN.

Then the last anchor of our hopes gives way!
He was the only man who dared to raise
His voice in favor of the people's rights.

KUNZ.

The storm grows worse and worse. So, fare ye well!
I'll go and seek out quarters in the village.
There's not a chance of getting off to-day.

[Exit.

FISHERMAN.

Tell dragged to prison, and the baron dead!
Now, tyranny, exalt thy insolent front—
Throw shame aside! The voice of truth is silenced,
The eye that watched for us in darkness closed,
The arm that should have struck thee down in chains!

BOY.

'Tis hailing hard—come, let us to the cottage
This is no weather to be out in, father!

FISHERMAN.

Rage on, ye winds! Ye lightnings, flash your fires!
Burst, ye swollen clouds! Ye cataracts of heaven,
Descend, and drown the country! In the germ,
Destroy the generations yet unborn!
Ye savage elements, be lords of all!
Return, ye bears; ye ancient wolves, return
To this wide, howling waste! The land is yours.
Who would live here when liberty is gone?

BOY.

Hark! How the wind whistles and the whirlpool roars;
I never saw a storm so fierce as this!

FISHERMAN.

To level at the head of his own child!
Never had father such command before.
And shall not nature, rising in wild wrath,
Revolt against the deed? I should not marvel,

Though to the lake these rocks should bow their heads,
Though yonder pinnacles, yon towers of ice,
That, since creation's dawn, have known no thaw,
Should, from their lofty summits, melt away;
Though yonder mountains, yon primeval cliffs,
Should topple down, and a new deluge whelm
Beneath its waves all living men's abodes!

[Bells heard.

BOY.
Hark! they are ringing on the mountain yonder!
They surely see some vessel in distress,
And toll the bell that we may pray for it.

[Ascends a rock.

FISHERMAN.
Woe to the bark that now pursues its course,
Rocked in the cradle of these storm-tossed waves.
Nor helm nor steersman here can aught avail;
The storm is master. Man is like a ball,
Tossed 'twixt the winds and billows. Far, or near,
No haven offers him its friendly shelter!
Without one ledge to grasp, the sheer, smooth rocks
Look down inhospitably on his despair,
And only tender him their flinty breasts.

BOY (calling from above).
Father, a ship; and bearing down from Flueelen.

FISHERMAN.
Heaven pity the poor wretches! When the storm
Is once entangled in this strait of ours,
It rages like some savage beast of prey,
Struggling against its cage's iron bars.
Howling, it seeks an outlet—all in vain;
For the rocks hedge it round on every side,
Walling the narrow pass as high as heaven.

[He ascends a cliff.

BOY.
It is the governor of Uri's ship;
By its red poop I know it, and the flag.

FISHERMAN.
Judgments of Heaven! Yes, it is he himself.
It is the governor! Yonder he sails,
And with him bears the burden of his crimes!
Soon has the arm of the avenger found him;
Now over him he knows a mightier lord.
These waves yield no obedience to his voice,
These rocks bow not their heads before his cap.
Boy, do not pray; stay not the Judge's arm!

BOY.
I pray not for the governor; I pray
For Tell, who is on board the ship with him.

FISHERMAN.
Alas, ye blind, unreasoning elements!
Must ye, in punishing one guilty head,
Destroy the vessel and the pilot too?

BOY.
See, see, they've cleared the Buggisgrat; but now
The blast, rebounding from the Devil's Minster,
Has driven them back on the Great Axenberg.
I cannot see them now.

FISHERMAN.
  The Hakmesser
Is there, that's foundered many a gallant ship.
If they should fail to double that with skill,
Their bark will go to pieces on the rocks
That hide their jagged peaks below the lake.
They have on board the very best of pilots;
If any man can save them, Tell is he;
But he is manacled, both hand and foot.

 [Enter WILLIAM TELL, with his crossbow. He enters
 precipitately, looks wildly round, and testifies the
 most violent agitation. When he reaches the centre
 of the stage, he throws himself upon his knees, and
 stretches out his hands, first towards the earth, then
 towards heaven.

BOY (observing him).
See, father! Who is that man, kneeling yonder?

FISHERMAN.

He clutches at the earth with both his hands,
And looks as though he were beside himself.

BOY (advancing).
What do I see? Father, come here, and look!

FISHERMAN (approaches).
Who is it? God in heaven! What! William Tell,
How came you hither? Speak, Tell!

BOY.
    Were you not
In yonder ship, a prisoner, and in chains?

FISHERMAN.
Were they not bearing you away to Kuessnacht?

TELL (rising).
I am released.

FISHERMAN and **BOY**.
  Released, oh miracle!

BOY.
Whence came you here?

TELL.
   From yonder vessel!

FISHERMAN.
   What?

BOY.
Where is the viceroy?

TELL.
   Drifting on the waves.

FISHERMAN.
Is't possible? But you! How are you here?
How 'scaped you from your fetters and the storm?

TELL.
By God's most gracious providence. Attend.

FISHERMAN and **BOY**.

Say on, say on!

TELL.

You know what passed at Altdorf?

FISHERMAN.

I do—say on!

TELL.

How I was seized and bound,
And ordered by the governor to Kuessnacht.

FISHERMAN.

And how with you at Flueelen he embarked.
All this we know. Say, how have you escaped?

TELL.

I lay on deck, fast bound with cords, disarmed,
In utter hopelessness. I did not think
Again to see the gladsome light of day,
Nor the dear faces of my wife and children;
And eyed disconsolate the waste of waters——

FISHERMAN.

Oh, wretched man!

TELL.

Then we put forth; the viceroy,
Rudolph der Harras, and their suite. My bow
And quiver lay astern beside the helm;
And just as we had reached the corner, near
The Little Axen, heaven ordained it so,
That from the Gotthardt's gorge, a hurricane
Swept down upon us with such headlong force,
That every rower's heart within him sank,
And all on board looked for a watery grave.
Then heard I one of the attendant train,
Turning to Gessler, in this strain accost him:
"You see our danger, and your own, my lord
And that we hover on the verge of death.
The boatmen there are powerless from fear,
Nor are they confident what course to take;
Now, here is Tell, a stout and fearless man,
And knows to steer with more than common skill.
How if we should avail ourselves of him
In this emergency?" The viceroy then

Addressed me thus: "If thou wilt undertake
To bring us through this tempest safely, Tell,
I might consent to free thee from thy bonds."
I answered, "Yes, my lord, with God's assistance,
I'll see what can be done, and help us heaven!"
On this they loosed me from my bonds, and I
Stood by the helm and fairly steered along;
Yet ever eyed my shooting-gear askance,
And kept a watchful eye upon the shore,
To find some point where I might leap to land
And when I had descried a shelving crag,
That jutted, smooth atop, into the lake——

FISHERMAN.
I know it. 'Tis at foot of the Great Axen;
But looks so steep, I never could have dreamed
'Twere possible to leap it from the boat.

TELL.
I bade the men put forth their utmost might,
Until we came before the shelving crag.
For there, I said, the danger will be past!
Stoutly they pulled, and soon we neared the point;
One prayer to God for his assisting grace,
And straining every muscle, I brought round
The vessel's stern close to the rocky wall;
Then snatching up my weapons, with a bound
I swung myself upon the flattened shelf,
And with my feet thrust off, with all my might,
The puny bark into the hell of waters.
There let it drift about, as heaven ordains!
Thus am I here, delivered from the might
Of the dread storm, and man, more dreadful still.

FISHERMAN.
Tell, Tell, the Lord has manifestly wrought
A miracle in thy behalf! I scarce
Can credit my own eyes. But tell me, now,
Whither you purpose to betake yourself?
For you will be in peril should the viceroy
Chance to escape this tempest with his life.

TELL.
I heard him say, as I lay bound on board,
His purpose was to disembark at Brunnen;
And, crossing Schwytz, convey me to his castle.

FISHERMAN.
Means he to go by land?

TELL.
So he intends.

FISHERMAN.
Oh, then, conceal yourself without delay!
Not twice will heaven release you from his grasp.

TELL.
Which is the nearest way to Arth and Kuessnacht?

FISHERMAN.
The public road leads by the way of Steinen,
But there's a nearer road, and more retired,
That goes by Lowerz, which my boy can show you.

TELL (gives him his hand).
May heaven reward your kindness! Fare ye well!

[As he is going he comes back.

Did not you also take the oath at Rootli?
I heard your name, methinks.

FISHERMAN.
Yes, I was there,
And took the oath of the confederacy;

TELL.
Then do me this one favor; speed to Buerglen
My wife is anxious at my absence—tell her
That I am free, and in secure concealment.

FISHERMAN.
But whither shall I tell her you have fled?

TELL.
You'll find her father with her, and some more,
Who took the oath with you upon the Rootli;
Bid them be resolute, and strong of heart,
For Tell is free and master of his arm;
They shall hear further news of me ere long.

FISHERMAN.

What have you, then, in view? Come, tell me frankly!

TELL.

When once 'tis done 'twill be in every mouth.

[Exit,

FISHERMAN.

Show him the way, boy. Heaven be his support!
Whate'er he has resolved, he'll execute.

[Exit,

SCENE II.

Baronial mansion of Attinghausen. The BARON upon a couch dying.
WALTER FURST, STAUFFACHER, MELCHTHAL, and
BAUMGARTEN attending round
him. WALTER TELL kneeling before the dying man.

FURST.

All now is over with him. He is gone.

STAUFFACHER.

He lies not like one dead. The feather, see,
Moves on his lips! His sleep is very calm,
And on his features plays a placid smile.

[BAUMGARTEN goes to the door and speaks with some one.

FURST.

Who's there?

BAUGMARTEN (returning).

Tell's wife, your daughter; she insists
That she must speak with you, and see her boy.

[**WALTER** TELL rises.

FURST.

I who need comfort—can I comfort her?

98

Does every sorrow centre on my head?

HEDWIG (forcing her way in).
Where is my child? Unhand me! I must see him.

STAUFFACHER.
Be calm! Reflect you're in the house of death!

HEDWIG (falling upon her boy's neck).
My Walter! Oh, he yet is mine!

WALTER.
      Dear mother!

HEDWIG.
And is it surely so? Art thou unhurt?

  [Gazing at him with anxious tenderness.

And is it possible he aimed at thee?
How could he do it? Oh, he has no heart—
And he could wing an arrow at his child!

FURST.
His soul was racked with anguish when he did it.
No choice was left him, but to shoot or die!

HEDWIG.
Oh, if he had a father's heart, he would
Have sooner perished by a thousand deaths!

STAUFFACHER.
You should be grateful for God's gracious care,
That ordered things so well.

HEDWIG.
      Can I forget
What might have been the issue. God of heaven!
Were I to live for centuries, I still
Should see my boy tied up,—his father's mark,
And still the shaft would quiver in my heart!

MELCHTHAL.
You know not how the viceroy taunted him!

HEDWIG.

Oh, ruthless heart of man! Offend his pride,
And reason in his breast forsakes her seat;
In his blind wrath he'll stake upon a cast
A child's existence, and a mother's heart!

BAUMGARTEN.
Is then your husband's fate not hard enough,
That you embitter it by such reproaches?
Have you no feeling for his sufferings?

HEDWIG (turning to him and gazing full upon him).
Hast thou tears only for thy friend's distress?
Say, where were you when he—my noble Tell,
Was bound in chains? Where was your friendship, then?
The shameful wrong was done before your eyes;
Patient you stood, and let your friend be dragged,
Ay, from your very hands. Did ever Tell
Act thus to you? Did he stand whining by
When on your heels the viceroy's horsemen pressed,
And full before you roared the storm-tossed lake?
Oh, not with idle tears he showed his pity;
Into the boat he sprung, forgot his home,
His wife, his children, and delivered thee!

FURST.
It had been madness to attempt his rescue,
Unarmed, and few in numbers as we were.

HEDWIG (casting herself upon his bosom).
Oh, father, and thou, too, hast lost my Tell!
The country—all have lost him! All lament
His loss; and, oh, how he must pine for us!
Heaven keep his soul from sinking to despair!
No friend's consoling voice can penetrate
His dreary dungeon walls. Should befall sick!
Ah! In the vapors of the murky vault
He must fall sick. Even as the Alpine rose
Grows pale and withers in the swampy air,
There is no life for him, but in the sun,
And in the balm of heaven's refreshing breeze.
Imprisoned? Liberty to him is breath;
He cannot live in the rank dungeon air!

STAUFFACHER.
Pray you be calm! And, hand in hand, we'll all
Combine to burst his prison doors.

HEDWIG.
      Without him,
What have you power to do? While Tell was free,
There still, indeed, was hope—weak innocence
Had still a friend, and the oppressed a stay.
Tell saved you all! You cannot all combined
Release him from his cruel prison bonds.

[The BARON wakes.

BAUMGARTEN.
Hush, hush! He starts!

ATTINGHAUSEN (sitting up).
      Where is he?

STAUFFACHER.
      Who?

ATTINGHAUSEN.
      He leaves me,—
In my last moments he abandons me.

STAUFFACHER.
He means his nephew. Have they sent for him?

FURST.
He has been summoned. Cheerily, Sir! Take comfort!
He has found his heart at last, and is our own.

ATTINGHAUSEN.
Say, has he spoken for his native land?

STAUFFACHER.
Ay, like a hero!

ATTINGHAUSEN.
      Wherefore comes he not,
That he may take my blessing ere I die?
I feel my life fast ebbing to a close.

STAUFFACHER.
Nay, talk not thus, dear Sir! This last short sleep
Has much refreshed you, and your eye is bright.

ATTINGHAUSEN.
Life is but pain, and even that has left me;
My sufferings, like my hopes, have passed away.

[Observing the boy.

What boy is that?

FURST.
Bless him. Oh, good my lord!
He is my grandson, and is fatherless.

[**HEDWIG** kneels with the boy before the dying man.

ATTINGHAUSEN.
And fatherless I leave you all, ay, all!
Oh, wretched fate, that these old eyes should see
My country's ruin, as they close in death.
Must I attain the utmost verge of life,
To feel my hopes go with me to the grave.

STAUFFACHER (to FURST).
Shall he depart 'mid grief and gloom like this?
Shall not his parting moments be illumed
By hope's delightful beams? My noble lord,
Raise up your drooping spirit! We are not
Forsaken quite—past all deliverance.

ATTINGHAUSEN.
Who shall deliver you?

FURST.
Ourselves. For know
The Cantons three are to each other pledged
To hunt the tyrants from the land. The league
Has been concluded, and a sacred oath
Confirms our union. Ere another year
Begins its circling course—the blow shall fall.
In a free land your ashes shall repose.

ATTINGHAUSEN.
The league concluded! Is it really so?

MELCHTHAL.
On one day shall the Cantons rise together.
All is prepared to strike—and to this hour

The secret closely kept though hundreds share it;
The ground is hollow 'neath the tyrant's feet;
Their days of rule are numbered, and ere long
No trace of their dominion shall remain.

ATTINGHAUSEN.
Ay, but their castles, how to master them?

MELCHTHAL.
On the same day they, too, are doomed to fall.

ATTINGHAUSEN.
And are the nobles parties to this league?

STAUFFACHER.
We trust to their assistance should we need it;
As yet the peasantry alone have sworn.

ATTINGHAUSEN (raising himself up in great astonishment).
And have the peasantry dared such a deed
On their own charge without their nobles' aid—
Relied so much on their own proper strength?
Nay then, indeed, they want our help no more;
We may go down to death cheered by the thought
That after us the majesty of man
Will live, and be maintained by other hands.

   [He lays his hand upon the head of the child,
   who is kneeling before him.

From this boy's head, whereon the apple lay,
Your new and better liberty shall spring;
The old is crumbling down—the times are changing
And from the ruins blooms a fairer life.

STAUFFACHER (to FURST).
See, see, what splendor streams around his eye!
This is not nature's last expiring flame,
It is the beam of renovated life.

ATTINGHAUSEN.
From their old towers the nobles are descending,
And swearing in the towns the civic oath.
In Uechtland and Thurgau the work's begun;
The noble Bern lifts her commanding head,
And Freyburg is a stronghold of the free;

The stirring Zurich calls her guilds to arms;
And now, behold! the ancient might of kings
Is shivered against her everlasting walls.

[He speaks what follows with a prophetic tone;
his utterance rising into enthusiasm.

I see the princes and their haughty peers,
Clad all in steel, come striding on to crush
A harmless shepherd race with mailed hand.
Desperate the conflict: 'tis for life or death;
And many a pass will tell to after years
Of glorious victories sealed in foemen's blood. 25
The peasant throws himself with naked breast,
A willing victim on their serried lances.
They yield—the flower of chivalry's cut down,
And freedom waves her conquering banner high!

[Grasps the hands Of WALTER FURST and STAUFFACHER.

Hold fast together, then—forever fast!
Let freedom's haunts be one in heart and mind!
Set watches on your mountain-tops, that league
May answer league, when comes the hour to strike.
Be one—be one—be one——

[He falls back upon the cushion. His lifeless hands continue
to grasp those of FURST and STAUFFACHER, who regard him for
some moments in silence, and then retire, overcome with sorrow.
Meanwhile the servants have quietly pressed into the chamber,
testifying different degrees of grief. Some kneel down beside
him and weep on his body: while this scene is passing the castle
bell tolls.

RUDENZ (entering hurriedly).
Lives he? Oh, say, can he still hear my voice?

FURST (averting his face).
You are our seignior and protector now;
Henceforth this castle bears another name.

RUDENZ (gazing at the body with deep emotion).
Oh, God! Is my repentance, then, too late?
Could he not live some few brief moments more,
To see the change that has come o'er my heart?
Oh, I was deaf to his true counselling voice

104

While yet he walked on earth. Now he is gone;
Gone and forever,—leaving me the debt,—
The heavy debt I owe him—undischarged!
Oh, tell me! did he part in anger with me?

STAUFFACHER.
When dying he was told what you had done,
And blessed the valor that inspired your words!

RUDENZ (kneeling downs beside the dead body).
Yes, sacred relics of a man beloved!
Thou lifeless corpse! Here, on thy death-cold hand,
Do I abjure all foreign ties forever!
And to my country's cause devote myself.
I am a Switzer, and will act as one
With my whole heart and soul.
    [Rises.
            Mourn for our friend,
Our common parent, yet be not dismayed!
'Tis not alone his lands that I inherit,—
His heart—his spirit have devolved on me;
And my young arm shall execute the task
For which his hoary age remained your debtor.
Give me your hands, ye venerable fathers!
Thine, Melchthal, too! Nay, do not hesitate,
Nor from me turn distrustfully away.
Accept my plighted vow—my knightly oath!

FURST.
Give him your hands, my friends! A heart like his
That sees and owns its error claims our trust.

MELCHTHAL.
You ever held the peasantry in scorn;
What surety have we that you mean us fair?

RUDENZ.
Oh, think not of the error of my youth!

STAUFFACHER (to MELCHTHAL).
Be one! They were our father's latest words.
See they be not forgotten! Take my hand,—
A peasant's hand,—and with it, noble Sir,
The gage and the assurance of a man!
Without us, sir, what would the nobles be?
Our order is more ancient, too, than yours!

RUDENZ.

I honor it, and with my sword will shield it!

MELCHTHAL.

The arm, my lord, that tames the stubborn earth,
And makes its bosom blossom with increase,
Can also shield a man's defenceless breast.

RUDENZ.

Then you shall shield my breast and I will yours;
Thus each be strengthened by the others' aid!
Yet wherefore talk we while our native land
Is still to alien tyranny a prey?
First let us sweep the foeman from the soil,
Then reconcile our difference in peace!

[After a moment's pause.

How! You are silent! Not a word for me?
And have I yet no title to your trust?
Then must I force my way, despite your will,
Into the league you secretly have formed.
You've held a Diet on the Rootli,—I
Know this,—know all that was transacted there!
And though I was not trusted with your secret,
I still have kept it like a sacred pledge.
Trust me, I never was my country's foe,
Nor would I ever have ranged myself against you!
Yet you did wrong to put your rising off.
Time presses! We must strike, and swiftly, too!
Already Tell has fallen a sacrifice
To your delay.

STAUFFACHER.

We swore to wait till Christmas.

RUDENZ.

I was not there,—I did not take the oath.
If you delay I will not!

MELCHTHAL.

What! You would——

RUDENZ.

I count me now among the country's fathers,

106

And to protect you is my foremost duty.

FURST.
Within the earth to lay these dear remains,
That is your nearest and most sacred duty.

RUDENZ.
When we have set the country free, we'll place
Our fresh, victorious wreaths upon his bier.
Oh, my dear friends, 'tis not your cause alone!
I have a cause to battle with the tyrants
That more concerns myself. Know, that my Bertha
Has disappeared,—been carried off by stealth,
Stolen from amongst us by their ruffian bands!

STAUFFACHER.
And has the tyrant dared so fell an outrage
Against a lady free and nobly born?

RUDENZ.
Alas! my friends, I promised help to you,
And I must first implore it for myself?
She that I love is stolen—is forced away,
And who knows where the tyrant has concealed her.
Or with what outrages his ruffian crew
May force her into nuptials she detests?
Forsake me not! Oh help me to her rescue!
She loves you! Well, oh well, has she deserved
That all should rush to arms in her behalf.

STAUFFACHER.
What course do you propose?

RUDENZ.
          Alas! I know not.
In the dark mystery that shrouds her fate,
In the dread agony of this suspense,
Where I can grasp at naught of certainty,
One single ray of comfort beams upon me.
From out the ruins of the tyrant's power
Alone can she be rescued from the grave.
Their strongholds must be levelled! Everyone,
Ere we can pierce into her gloomy prison.

MELCHTHAL.
Come, lead us on! We follow! Why defer

Until to-morrow what to-day may do?
Tell's arm was free when we at Rootli swore,
This foul enormity was yet undone.
And change of circumstance brings change of law.
Who such a coward as to waver still?

RUDENZ (to WALTER FURST).
Meanwhile to arms, and wait in readiness
The fiery signal on the mountain-tops.
For swifter than a boat can scour the lake
Shall you have tidings of our victory;
And when you see the welcome flames ascend,
Then, like the lightning, swoop upon the foe,
And lay the despots and their creatures low!

SCENE III.

The pass near Kuessnacht, sloping down from behind, with
rocks on either side. The travellers are visible upon the
heights, before they appear on the stage. Rocks all round
the stage. Upon one of the foremost a projecting cliff
overgrown with brushwood.

TELL (enters with his crossbow).
Here through this deep defile he needs must pass;
There leads no other road to Kuessnacht; here
I'll do it; the opportunity is good.
Yon alder tree stands well for my concealment,
Thence my avenging shaft will surely reach him.
The straitness of the path forbids pursuit.
Now, Gessler, balance thine account with Heaven!
Thou must away from earth, thy sand is run.
I led a peaceful, inoffensive life;
My bow was bent on forest game alone,
And my pure soul was free from thoughts of murder.
But thou hast scared me from my dream of peace;
The milk of human kindness thou hast turned
To rankling poison in my breast, and made
Appalling deeds familiar to my soul.
He who could make his own child's head his mark
Can speed his arrow to his foeman's heart.

My children dear, my loved and faithful wife,
Must be protected, tyrant, from thy fury!
When last I drew my bow, with trembling hand,
And thou, with murderous joy, a father forced
To level at his child; when, all in vain,
Writhing before thee, I implored thy mercy,
Then in the agony of my soul I vowed
A fearful oath, which met God's ear alone,
That when my bow next winged an arrow's flight
Its aim should be thy heart. The vow I made
Amid the hellish torments of that moment
I hold a sacred debt, and I will pay it.

Thou art my lord, my emperor's delegate,
Yet would the emperor not have stretched his power
So far as thou. He sent thee to these Cantons
To deal forth law, stern law, for he is angered;
But not to wanton with unbridled will
In every cruelty, with fiendlike joy:
There is a God to punish and avenge.

Come forth, thou bringer once of bitter pangs,
My precious jewel now, my chiefest treasure;
A mark I'll set thee, which the cry of grief
Could never penetrate, but thou shalt pierce it.
And thou, my trusty bowstring, that so oft
Has served me faithfully in sportive scenes,
Desert me not in this most serious hour—
Only be true this once, my own good cord,
That has so often winged the biting shaft:—
For shouldst thou fly successless from my hand,
I have no second to send after thee.

[Travellers pass over the stage.

I'll sit me down upon this bench of stone,
Hewn for the wayworn traveller's brief repose—
For here there is no home. Each hurries by
The other, with quick step and careless look,
Nor stays to question of his grief. Here goes
The merchant, full of care—the pilgrim next,
With slender scrip—and then the pious monk,
The scowling robber, and the jovial player,
The carrier with his heavy-laden horse,
That comes to us from the far haunts of men;
For every road conducts to the world's end.

109

They all push onwards—every man intent
On his own several business—mine is murder.

   [Sits down.

Time was, my dearest children, when with joy
You hailed your father's safe return to home
From his long mountain toils; for when he came
He ever brought some little present with him.
A lovely Alpine flower—a curious bird—
Or elf-boat found by wanderers on the hills.
But now he goes in quest of other game:
In the wild pass he sits, and broods on murder;
And watches for the life-blood of his foe,
But still his thoughts are fixed on you alone,
Dear children. 'Tis to guard your innocence,
To shield you from the tyrant's fell revenge,
He bends his bow to do a deed of blood!

   [Rises.

Well—I am watching for a noble prey—
Does not the huntsman, with severest toil,
Roam for whole days amid the winter's cold,
Leap with a daring bound from rock to rock,—
And climb the jagged, slippery steeps, to which
His limbs are glued by his own streaming blood;
And all this but to gain a wretched chamois.
A far more precious prize is now my aim—
The heart of that dire foe who would destroy me.

   [Sprightly music heard in the distance, which
   comes gradually nearer.

From my first years of boyhood I have used
The bow—been practised in the archer's feats;
The bull's-eye many a time my shafts have hit,
And many a goodly prize have I brought home,
Won in the games of skill. This day I'll make
My master-shot, and win the highest prize
Within the whole circumference of the mountains.

   [A marriage train passes over the stage, and goes up
   the pass. TELL gazes at it, leaning on his bow. He
   is joined by STUSSI, the Ranger.

110

STUSSI.

There goes the bridal party of the steward
Of Moerlischachen's cloister. He is rich!
And has some ten good pastures on the Alps.
He goes to fetch his bride from Imisee,
There will be revelry to-night at Kuessnacht.
Come with us—every honest man's invited.

TELL.

A gloomy guest fits not a wedding feast.

STUSSI.

If grief oppress you, dash it from your heart!
Bear with your lot. The times are heavy now,
And we must snatch at pleasure while we can.
Here 'tis a bridal, there a burial.

TELL.

And oft the one treads close upon the other.

STUSSI.

So runs the world at present. Everywhere
We meet with woe and misery enough.
There's been a slide of earth in Glarus, and
A whole side of the Glaernisch has fallen in.

TELL.

Strange! And do even the hills begin to totter?
There is stability for naught on earth.

STUSSI.

Strange tidings, too, we hear from other parts.
I spoke with one but now, that came from Baden,
Who said a knight was on his way to court,
And as he rode along a swarm of wasps
Surrounded him, and settling on his horse,
So fiercely stung the beast that it fell dead,
And he proceeded to the court on foot.

TELL.

Even the weak are furnished with a sting.

[**ARMGART** (enters with several children, and places
herself at the entrance of the pass).

STUSSI.

'Tis thought to bode disaster to the country,
Some horrid deed against the course of nature.

TELL.
Why, every day brings forth such fearful deeds;
There needs no miracle to tell their coming.

STUSSI.
Too true! He's blessed who tills his field in peace,
And sits untroubled by his own fireside.

TELL.
The very meekest cannot rest in quiet,
Unless it suits with his ill neighbor's humor.

[TELL looks frequently with restless expectation
towards the top of the pass.

STUSSI.
So fare you well! You're waiting some one here?

TELL.
I am.

STUSSI.
    A pleasant meeting with your friends!
You are from Uri, are you not? His grace
The governor's expected thence to-day.

TRAVELLER (entering).
Look not to see the governor to-day.
The streams are flooded by the heavy rains,
And all the bridges have been swept away.

[TELL rises.

ARMGART (coming forward).
The viceroy not arrived?

STUSSI.
        And do you seek him?

ARMGART.
Alas, I do!

STUSSI.

But why thus place yourself
Where you obstruct his passage down the pass?

ARMGART.
Here he cannot escape me. He must hear me.

FRIESSHARDT (coming hastily down the pass, and calls upon the stage).
Make way, make way! My lord, the governor,
Is coming down on horseback close behind me.

[Exit TELL.

ARMGART (with animation).
The viceroy comes!

[She goes towards the pass with her children.
GESSLER and RUDOLPH DER HARRAS appear upon the
heights on horseback.

STUSSI (to FRIESSHARDT).
How got ye through the stream
When all the bridges have been carried down?

FRIESSHARDT.
We've battled with the billows; and, my friend,
An Alpine torrent's nothing after that.

STUSSI.
How! Were you out, then, in that dreadful storm?

FRIESSHARDT.
Ay, that we were! I shall not soon forget it.

STUSSI.
Stay, speak——

FRIESSHARDT.
I cannot. I must to the castle,
And tell them that the governor's at hand.

[Exit.

STUSSI.
If honest men, now, had been in the ship,
It had gone down with every soul on board:—
Some folks are proof 'gainst fire and water both.

[Looking round.

Where has the huntsman gone with whom I spoke?

[Exit.

Enter GESSLER and RUDOLPH DER HARRAS on horseback.

GESSLER.
Say what you please; I am the emperor's servant,
And my first care must be to do his pleasure.
He did not send me here to fawn and cringe
And coax these boors into good humor. No!
Obedience he must have. We soon shall see
If king or peasant is to lord it here?

ARMGART.
Now is the moment! Now for my petition!

GESSLER.
'Twas not in sport that I set up the cap
In Altdorf—or to try the people's hearts—
All this I knew before. I set it up
That they might learn to bend those stubborn necks
They carry far too proudly—and I placed
What well I knew their eyes could never brook
Full in the road, which they perforce must pass,
That, when their eyes fell on it, they might call
That lord to mind whom they too much forget.

HARRAS.
But surely, sir, the people have some rights——

GESSLER.
This is no time to settle what they are.
Great projects are at work, and hatching now;
The imperial house seeks to extend its power.
Those vast designs of conquests, which the sire
Has gloriously begun, the son will end.
This petty nation is a stumbling-block—
One way or other it must be subjected.

[They are about to pass on. ARMMGART throws herself
down before GESSLER.

114

ARMGART.
Mercy, lord governor! Oh, pardon, pardon!

GESSLER.
Why do you cross me on the public road?
Stand back, I say.

ARMGART.
  My husband lies in prison;
My wretched orphans cry for bread. Have pity,
Pity, my lord, upon our sore distress!

HARRAS.
Who are you, woman; and who is your husband?

ARMGART.
A poor wild hay-man of the Rigiberg,
Kind sir, who on the brow of the abyss,
Mows down the grass from steep and craggy shelves,
To which the very cattle dare not climb.

HARRAS (to **GESSLER**).
By Heaven! a sad and miserable life!
I prithee, give the wretched man his freedom.
How great soever his offence may be,
His horrid trade is punishment enough.

  [To ARMGART.

You shall have justice. To the castle bring
Your suit. This is no place to deal with it.

ARMGART.
No, no, I will not stir from where I stand,
Until your grace restore my husband to me.
Six months already has he been in prison,
And waits the sentence of a judge in vain.

GESSLER.
How! Would you force me, woman? Hence! Begone!

ARMGART.
Justice, my lord! Ay, justice! Thou art judge!
The deputy of the emperor—of Heaven!
Then do thy duty, as thou hopest for justice
From Him who rules above, show it to us!

115

GESSLER.
Hence! drive this daring rabble from my sight!

ARMGART (seizing his horse's reins).
No, no, by Heaven, I've nothing more to lose.
Thou stirrest not, viceroy, from this spot until
Thou dost me fullest justice. Knit thy brows,
And roll thy eyes; I fear not. Our distress
Is so extreme, so boundless, that we care
No longer for thine anger.

GESSLER.
      Woman, hence!
Give way, I say, or I will ride thee down.

ARMGART.
Well, do so; there!

   [Throws her children and herself upon the ground before him.

      Here on the ground I lie,
I and my children. Let the wretched orphans
Be trodden by thy horse into the dust!
It will not be the worst that thou hast done.

HARRAS.
Are you mad, woman?

ARMGART (continuing with vehemence).
      Many a day thou hast
Trampled the emperor's lands beneath thy feet.
Oh, I am but a woman! Were I man,
I'd find some better thing to do, than here
Lie grovelling in the dust.

   [The music of the wedding party is again heard
   from the top of the pass, but more softly.

GESSLER.
      Where are my knaves?
Drag her away, lest I forget myself,
And do some deed I may repent hereafter.

HARRAS.
My lord, the servants cannot force a passage;

The pass is blocked up by a marriage party.

GESSLER.
Too mild a ruler am I to this people,
Their tongues are all too bold; nor have they yet
Been tamed to due submission, as they shall be.
I must take order for the remedy;
I will subdue this stubborn mood of theirs,
And crush the soul of liberty within them.
I'll publish a new law throughout the land;
I will——

[An arrow pierces him,—he puts his hand on his heart,
and is about to sink—with a feeble voice.

Oh God, have mercy on my soul!

HARRAS.
My lord! my lord! Oh God! What's this? Whence came it?

ARMGART (starts up).
Dead, dead! He reels, he falls! 'Tis in his heart!

HARRAS (springs from his horse).
This is most horrible! Oh Heavens! sir knight,
Address yourself to God and pray for mercy;
You are a dying man.

GESSLER.
　　　That shot was Tell's.

[He slides from his horse into the arms of RUDOLPH
DER HARRAS, who lays him down upon the bench. TELL
appears above, upon the rocks.

TELL.
Thou knowest the archer, seek no other hand.
Our cottages are free, and innocence
Secure from thee: thou'lt be our curse no more.

[TELL disappears. People rush in.

117

STUSSI.
What is the matter? Tell me what has happened?

ARMGART.
The governor is shot,—killed by an arrow!

PEOPLE (running in).
Who has been shot?

> [While the foremost of the marriage party are coming
> on the stage, the hindmost are still upon the heights.
> The music continues.

HARRAS.
     He's bleeding fast to death.
Away, for help—pursue the murderer!
Unhappy man, is't thus that thou must die?
Thou wouldst not heed the warnings that I gave thee!

STUSSI.
By heaven, his cheek is pale! His life ebbs fast.

MANY VOICES.
Who did the deed?

HARRAS.
     What! Are the people mad
That they make music to a murder? Silence!

> [Music breaks off suddenly. People continue to flock in.

Speak, if thou canst, my lord. Hast thou no charge
To intrust me with?

> [GESSLER makes signs with his hand, which he repeats
> with vehemence, when he finds they are not understood.

     What would you have me do?
Shall I to Kuessnacht? I can't guess your meaning.
Do not give way to this impatience. Leave
All thoughts of earth and make your peace with Heaven.

> [The whole marriage party gather round the dying man.

STUSSI.

See there! how pale he grows! Death's gathering now
About his heart; his eyes grow dim and glazed.

ARMGART (holds up a child).
Look, children, how a tyrant dies!

HARRAS.
         Mad hag!
Have you no touch of feeling that you look
On horrors such as these without a shudder?
Help me—take hold. What, will not one assist
To pull the torturing arrow from his breast?

WOMEN.
We touch the man whom God's own hand has struck!

HARRAS.
All curses light on you!

    [Draws his sword.

STUSSI (seizes his arm).
         Gently, sir knight!
Your power is at an end. 'Twere best forbear.
Our country's foe is fallen. We will brook
No further violence. We are free men.

ALL.
The country's free!

HARRAS.
         And is it come to this?
Fear and obedience at an end so soon?

    [To the soldiers of the guard who are thronging in.

You see, my friends, the bloody piece of work
They've acted here. 'Tis now too late for help,
And to pursue the murderer were vain.
New duties claim our care. Set on to Kuessnacht,
And let us save that fortress for the king!
For in an hour like this all ties of order,
Fealty, and faith are scattered to the winds.
No man's fidelity is to be trusted.

    [As he is going out with the soldiers six

FRATRES MISERICCRDIAE appear.

ARMGART.
Here come the brotherhood of mercy. Room!

STUSSI.
The victim's slain, and now the ravens stoop.

BROTHERS OF MERCY (form a semicircle round the body, and sing in solemn tones).

With hasty step death presses on,
 Nor grants to man a moment's stay,
He falls ere half his race be run
 In manhood's pride is swept away!
Prepared or unprepared to die,
He stands before his Judge on high.

[While they are repeating the last two lines, the curtain falls.

ACT V.

SCENE I.

A common near Altdorf. In the background to the right the keep
of Uri, with the scaffold still standing, as in the third scene
of the first act. To the left the view opens upon numerous
mountains, on all of which signal fires are burning. Day is
breaking, and bells are heard ringing from various distances.

RUODI, KUONI, WERNI, MASTER MASON, and many other country
people,
 also women and children.

RUODI.
Look at the fiery signals on the mountains!

120

MASTER MASON.
Hark to the bells above the forest there!

RUODI.
The enemy's expelled.

MASTER MASON.
⠀⠀⠀⠀The forts are taken.

RUODI.
And we of Uri, do we still endure
Upon our native soil the tyrant's keep?
Are we the last to strike for liberty?

MASTER MASON.
Shall the yoke stand that was to bow our necks?
Up! Tear it to the ground!

ALL.
⠀⠀⠀⠀Down, down with it!

RUODI.
Where is the Stier of Uri?

URI.
⠀⠀⠀⠀Here. What would ye?

RUODI.
Up to your tower, and wind us such a blast,
As shall resound afar, from hill to hill;
Rousing the echoes of each peak and glen,
And call the mountain men in haste together!

⠀⠀[Exit STIER OF URI—enter WALTER FURST.

FURST.
Stay, stay, my friends! As yet we have not learned
What has been done in Unterwald and Schwytz.
Let's wait till we receive intelligence!

RUODI.
Wait, wait for what? The accursed tyrant's dead,
And the bright day of liberty has dawned!

MASTER MASON.
How! Do these flaming signals not suffice,

That blaze on every mountain top around?

RUODI.
Come all, fall to—come, men and women, all!
Destroy the scaffold! Tear the arches down!
Down with the walls; let not a stone remain.

MASTER MASON.
Come, comrades, come! We built it, and we know
How best to hurl it down.

ALL.
      Come! Down with it!

[They fall upon the building at every side.

FURST.
The floodgate's burst. They're not to be restrained.

[Enter MELCHTHAL and BAUMGARTEN.

MELCHTHAL.
What! Stands the fortress still, when Sarnen lies
In ashes, and when Rossberg is a ruin?

FURST.
You, Melchthal, here? D'ye bring us liberty?
Say, have you freed the country of the foe?

MELCHTHAL.
We've swept them from the soil. Rejoice, my friend;
Now, at this very moment, while we speak,
There's not a tyrant left in Switzerland!

FURST.
How did you get the forts into your power?

MELCHTHAL.
Rudenz it was who with a gallant arm,
And manly daring, took the keep at Sarnen.
The Rossberg I had stormed the night before.
But hear what chanced. Scarce had we driven the foe
Forth from the keep, and given it to the flames,
That now rose crackling upwards to the skies,
When from the blaze rushed Diethelm, Gessler's page,
Exclaiming, "Lady Bertha will be burnt!"

122

FURST.
Good heavens!

[The beams of the scaffold are heard falling.

MELCHTHAL.
'Twas she herself. Here had she been
Immured in secret by the viceroy's orders.
Rudenz sprang up in frenzy. For we heard
The beams and massive pillars crashing down,
And through the volumed smoke the piteous shrieks
Of the unhappy lady.

FURST.
Is she saved?

MELCHTHAL.
Here was a time for promptness and decision!
Had he been nothing but our baron, then
We should have been most chary of our lives;
But he was our confederate, and Bertha
Honored the people. So without a thought,
We risked the worst, and rushed into the flames.

FURST.
But is she saved?

MELCHTHAL.
She is. Rudenz and I
Bore her between us from the blazing pile,
With crashing timbers toppling all around.
And when she had revived, the danger past,
And raised her eyes to meet the light of heaven,
The baron fell upon my breast; and then
A silent vow of friendship passed between us—
A vow that, tempered in yon furnace heat,
Will last through every shock of time and fate.

FURST.
Where is the Landenberg?

MELCHTHAL.
Across the Bruenig.
No fault of mine it was, that he, who quenched
My father's eyesight, should go hence unharmed.

He fled—I followed—overtook and seized him,
And dragged him to my father's feet. The sword
Already quivered o'er the caitiff's head,
When at the entreaty of the blind old man,
I spared the life for which he basely prayed.
He swore Urphede 26, never to return:
He'll keep his oath, for he has felt our arm.

FURST.
Thank God, our victory's unstained by blood!

CHILDREN (running across the stage with fragments of wood).
Liberty! Liberty! Hurrah, we're free!

FURST.
Oh! what a joyous scene! These children will,
E'en to their latest day, remember it.

   [Girls bring in the cap upon a pole. The whole stage
   is filled with people.

RUODI.
Here is the cap, to which we were to bow!

BAUMGARTEN.
Command us, how we shall dispose of it.

FURST.
Heavens! 'Twas beneath this cap my grandson stood!

SEVERAL VOICES.
Destroy the emblem of the tyrant's power!
Let it burn!

FURST.
    No. Rather be preserved!
'Twas once the instrument of despots—now
'Twill be a lasting symbol of our freedom.

   [Peasants, men, women, and children, some standing,
   others sitting upon the beams of the shattered scaffold,
   all picturesquely grouped, in a large semicircle.

MELCHTHAL.
Thus now, my friends, with light and merry hearts,
We stand upon the wreck of tyranny;

124

And gallantly have we fulfilled the oath,
Which we at Rootli swore, confederates!

FURST.
The work is but begun. We must be firm.
For, be assured, the king will make all speed,
To avenge his viceroy's death, and reinstate,
By force of arms, the tyrant we've expelled.

MELCHTHAL.
Why, let him come, with all his armaments!
The foe within has fled before our arms;
We'll give him welcome warmly from without!

RUODI.
The passes to the country are but few;
And these we'll boldly cover with our bodies.

BAUMGARTEN.
We are bound by an indissoluble league,
And all his armies shall not make us quail.

[Enter ROSSELMANN and STAUFFACHER.

ROSSELMANN (speaking as he enters).
These are the awful judgments of the lord!

PEASANT.
What is the matter?

ROSSELMANN.
In what times we live!

FURST.
Say on, what is't? Ha, Werner, is it you?
What tidings?

PEASANT.
What's the matter?

ROSSELMANN.
Hear and wonder.

STAUFFACHER.
We are released from one great cause of dread.

125

ROSSELMANN.
The emperor is murdered.

FURST.
      Gracious heaven!

[**PEASANTS** rise up and throng round STAUFFACHER.

ALL.
Murdered! the emperor? What! The emperor! Hear!

MELCHTHAL.
Impossible! How came you by the news?

STAUFFACHER.
'Tis true! Near Bruck, by the assassin's hand,
King Albert fell. A most trustworthy man,
John Mueller, from Schaffhausen, brought the news.

FURST.
Who dared commit so horrible a deed?

STAUFFACHER.
The doer makes the deed more dreadful still;
It was his nephew, his own brother's child,
Duke John of Austria, who struck the blow.

MELCHTHAL.
What drove him to so dire a parricide?

STAUFFACHER.
The emperor kept his patrimony back,
Despite his urgent importunities;
'Twas said, indeed, he never meant to give it,
But with a mitre to appease the duke.
However this may be, the duke gave ear,
To the ill counsel of his friends in arms;
And with the noble lords, von Eschenbach,
Von Tegerfeld, von Wart, and Palm, resolved,
Since his demands for justice were despised,
With his own hands to take revenge at least.

FURST.
But say, how compassed he the dreadful deed?

STAUFFACHER.

The king was riding down from Stein to Baden,
Upon his way to join the court at Rheinfeld,—
With him a train of high-born gentlemen,
And the young princes, John and Leopold.
And when they reached the ferry of the Reuss,
The assassins forced their way into the boat,
To separate the emperor from his suite.
His highness landed, and was riding on
Across a fresh-ploughed field—where once, they say,
A mighty city stood in Pagan times—
With Hapsburg's ancient turrets full in sight,
Where all the grandeur of his line had birth—
When Duke John plunged a dagger in his throat,
Palm ran him through the body with his lance,
Eschenbach cleft his skull at one fell blow,
And down he sank, all weltering in his blood,
On his own soil, by his own kinsmen slain.
Those on the opposite bank, who saw the deed,
Being parted by the stream, could only raise
An unavailing cry of loud lament.
But a poor woman, sitting by the way,
Raised him, and on her breast he bled to death.

MELCHTHAL.
Thus has he dug his own untimely grave,
Who sought insatiably to grasp at all.

STAUFFACHER.
The country round is filled with dire alarm.
The mountain passes are blockaded all,
And sentinels on every frontier set;
E'en ancient Zurich barricades her gates,
That for these thirty years have open stood,
Dreading the murderers, and the avengers more,
For cruel Agnes comes, the Hungarian queen,
To all her sex's tenderness a stranger,
Armed with the thunders of the church to wreak
Dire vengeance for her parent's royal blood,
On the whole race of those that murdered him,—
Upon their servants, children, children's children,—
Nay on the stones that build their castle walls.
Deep has she sworn a vow to immolate
Whole generations on her father's tomb,
And bathe in blood as in the dew of May.

MELCHTHAL.

Know you which way the murderers have fled?

STAUFFACHER.
No sooner had they done the deed than they
Took flight, each following a different route,
And parted, ne'er to see each other more.
Duke John must still be wandering in the mountains.

FURST.
And thus their crime has yielded them no fruits.
Revenge is barren. Of itself it makes
The dreadful food it feeds on; its delight
Is murder—its satiety despair.

STAUFFACHER.
The assassins reap no profit by their crime;
But we shall pluck with unpolluted hands
The teeming fruits of their most bloody deed,
For we are ransomed from our heaviest fear;
The direst foe of liberty has fallen,
And, 'tis reported, that the crown will pass
From Hapsburg's house into another line.
The empire is determined to assert
Its old prerogative of choice, I hear.

FURST and several others.
Has any one been named to you?

STAUFFACHER.
         The Count
Of Luxembourg is widely named already.

FURST.
'Tis well we stood so stanchly by the empire!
Now we may hope for justice, and with cause.

STAUFFACHER.
The emperor will need some valiant friends,
And he will shelter us from Austria's vengeance.

[The peasantry embrace. Enter SACRIST, with imperial messenger.

SACRIST.
Here are the worthy chiefs of Switzerland!

ROSSELMANN and several others.

128

Sacrist, what news?

SACRISTAN.
A courier brings this letter.

ALL (to **WALTER** FURST).
Open and read it.

FURST (reading).
"To the worthy men
Of Uri, Schwytz, and Unterwald, the Queen
Elizabeth sends grace and all good wishes!"

MANY VOICES.
What wants the queen with us? Her reign is done.

FURST (reads).
"In the great grief and doleful widowhood,
In which the bloody exit of her lord
Has plunged her majesty, she still remembers
The ancient faith and love of Switzerland."

MELCHTHAL.
She ne'er did that in her prosperity.

ROSSELMANN.
Hush, let us hear.

FURST (reads).
"And she is well assured,
Her people will in due abhorrence hold
The perpetrators of this damned deed.
On the three Cantons, therefore, she relies,
That they in nowise lend the murderers aid;
But rather, that they loyally assist
To give them up to the avenger's hand,
Remembering the love and grace which they
Of old received from Rudolph's princely house."

[Symptoms of dissatisfaction among the peasantry.

MANY VOICES.
The love and grace!

STAUFFACHER.
Grace from the father we, indeed, received,

But what have we to boast of from the son?
Did he confirm the charter of our freedom,
As all preceding emperors had done?
Did he judge righteous judgment, or afford
Shelter or stay to innocence oppressed?
Nay, did he e'en give audience to the envoys
We sent to lay our grievances before him?
Not one of all these things e'er did the king.
And had we not ourselves achieved our rights
By resolute valor our necessities
Had never touched him. Gratitude to him!
Within these vales he sowed not gratitude.
He stood upon an eminence—he might
Have been a very father to his people,
But all his aim and pleasure was to raise
Himself and his own house: and now may those
Whom he has aggrandized lament for him!

FURST.
We will not triumph in his fall, nor now
Recall to mind the wrongs we have endured.
Far be't from us! Yet, that we should avenge
The sovereign's death, who never did us good,
And hunt down those who ne'er molested us,
Becomes us not, nor is our duty. Love
Must bring its offerings free and unconstrained;
From all enforced duties death absolves—
And unto him we are no longer bound.

MELCHTHAL.
And if the queen laments within her bower,
Accusing heaven in sorrow's wild despair;
Here see a people from its anguish freed.
To that same heaven send up its thankful praise,
For who would reap regrets must sow affection.

[Exit the imperial courier.

STAUFFACHER (to the people).
But where is Tell? Shall he, our freedom's founder,
Alone be absent from our festival?
He did the most—endured the worst of all.
Come—to his dwelling let us all repair,
And bid the savior of our country hail!

[Exeunt omnes.

130

SCENE II.

Interior of TELL'S cottage. A fire burning on the hearth.
The open door shows the scene outside.

HEDWIG, WALTER, and WILHELM.

HEDWIG.
Boys, dearest boys! your father comes to-day.
He lives, is free, and we and all are free!
The country owes its liberty to him!

WALTER.
And I too, mother, bore my part in it;
I shall be named with him. My father's shaft
Went closely by my life, but yet I shook not!

HEDWIG (embracing him).
Yes, yes, thou art restored to me again.
Twice have I given thee birth, twice suffered all
A mother's agonies for thee, my child!
But this is past; I have you both, boys, both!
And your dear father will be back to-day.

[A monk appears at the door.

WILHELM.
See, mother, yonder stands a holy friar;
He's asking alms, no doubt.

HEDWIG.
          Go lead him in,
That we may give him cheer, and make him feel
That he has come into the house of joy.

[Exit, and returns immediately with a cup.

WILHELM (to the monk).
Come in, good man. Mother will give you food.

WALTER.

131

Come in, and rest, then go refreshed away!

MONK (glancing round in terror, with unquiet looks).
Where am I? In what country?

WALTER.
       Have you lost
Your way, that you are ignorant of this?
You are at Buerglen, in the land of Uri,
Just at the entrance of the Sheckenthal.

MONK (to HEDWIG).
Are you alone? Your husband, is he here?

HEDWIG.
I momently expect him. But what ails you?
You look as one whose soul is ill at ease.
Whoe'er you be, you are in want; take that.

[Offers him the cup.

MONK.
Howe'er my sinking heart may yearn for food,
I will take nothing till you've promised me——

HEDWIG.
Touch not my dress, nor yet advance one step.
Stand off, I say, if you would have me hear you.

MONK.
Oh, by this hearth's bright, hospitable blaze,
By your dear children's heads, which I embrace——

[Grasps the boys.

HEDWIG.
Stand back, I say! What is your purpose, man?
Back from my boys! You are no monk,—no, no.
Beneath that robe content and peace should dwell,
But neither lives within that face of thine.

MONK.
I am the veriest wretch that breathes on earth.

HEDWIG.
The heart is never deaf to wretchedness;

132

But thy look freezes up my inmost soul.

WALTER (springs up).
Mother, my father!

HEDWIG.
> Oh, my God!

[Is about to follow, trembles and stops.

WILHELM (running after his brother).
My father!

WALTER (without).
Thou'rt here once more!

WILHELM (without).
> My father, my dear father!

TELL (without).
Yes, here I am once more! Where is your mother?

[They enter.

WALTER.
There at the door she stands, and can no further,
She trembles so with terror and with joy.

TELL.
Oh Hedwig, Hedwig, mother of my children!
God has been kind and helpful in our woes.
No tyrant's hand shall e'er divide us more.

HEDWIG (falling on his neck).
Oh, Tell, what have I suffered for thy sake!

[Monk becomes attentive.

TELL.
Forget it now, and live for joy alone!
I'm here again with you! This is my cot
I stand again on mine own hearth!

WILHELM.
> But, father,
Where is your crossbow left? I see it not.

TELL.
Nor shalt thou ever see it more, my boy.
It is suspended in a holy place,
And in the chase shall ne'er be used again.

HEDWIG.
Oh, Tell, Tell!

[Steps back, dropping his hand.

TELL.
What alarms thee, dearest wife?

HEDWIG.
How—how dost thou return to me? This hand—
Dare I take hold of it? This hand—Oh God!

TELL (with firmness and animation).
Has shielded you and set my country free;
Freely I raise it in the face of Heaven.

[MONK gives a sudden start—he looks at him.

Who is this friar here?

HEDWIG.
Ah, I forgot him.
Speak thou with him; I shudder at his presence.

MONK (stepping nearer).
Are you that Tell that slew the governor?

TELL.
Yes, I am he. I hide the fact from no man.

MONK.
You are that Tell! Ah! it is God's own hand
That hath conducted me beneath your roof.

TELL (examining him closely).
You are no monk. Who are you?

MONK.
You have slain
The governor, who did you wrong. I too,

134

Have slain a foe, who late denied me justice.
He was no less your enemy than mine.
I've rid the land of him.

TELL (drawing back).
      Thou art—oh horror!
In—children, children—in without a word.
Go, my dear wife! Go! Go! Unhappy man,
Thou shouldst be——

HEIWIG.
Heavens, who is it?

TELL.
      Do not ask.
Away! away! the children must not hear it.
Out of the house—away! Thou must not rest
'Neath the same roof with this unhappy man!

HEDWIG.
Alas! What is it? Come!

   [Exit with the children.

TELL (to the MONK).
      Thou art the Duke
Of Austria—I know it. Thou hast slain
The emperor, thy uncle, and liege lord.

DUKE JOHN.
He robbed me of my patrimony.

TELL.
      How!
Slain him—thy king, thy uncle! And the earth
Still bears thee! And the sun still shines on thee!

DUKE JOHN.
Tell, hear me, ere you——

TELL.
      Reeking with the blood
Of him that was thy emperor and kinsman,
Durst thou set foot within my spotless house?
Show thy fell visage to a virtuous man,
And claim the rites of hospitality?

DUKE JOHN.

I hoped to find compassion at your hands.
You also took revenge upon your foe!

TELL.

Unhappy man! And dar'st thou thus confound
Ambition's bloody crime with the dread act
To which a father's direful need impelled him?
Hadst thou to shield thy children's darling heads?
To guard thy fireside's sanctuary—ward off
The last, worst doom from all that thou didst love?
To heaven I raise my unpolluted hands,
To curse thine act and thee! I have avenged
That holy nature which thou hast profaned.
I have no part with thee. Thou art a murderer;
I've shielded all that was most dear to me.

DUKE JOHN.

You cast me off to comfortless despair!

TELL.

My blood runs cold even while I talk with thee.
Away! Pursue thine awful course! Nor longer
Pollute the cot where innocence abides!

[DUKE JOHN turns to depart.

DUKE JOHN.

I cannot live, and will no longer thus!

TELL.

And yet my soul bleeds for thee—gracious heaven!
So young, of such a noble line, the grandson
Of Rudolph, once my lord and emperor,
An outcast—murderer—standing at my door,
The poor man's door—a suppliant, in despair!

[Covers his face.

DUKE JOHN.

If thou hast power to weep, oh let my fate
Move your compassion—it is horrible.
I am—say, rather was—a prince. I might
Have been most happy had I only curbed
The impatience of my passionate desires;

But envy gnawed my heart—I saw the youth
Of mine own cousin Leopold endowed
With honor, and enriched with broad domains,
The while myself, that was in years his equal,
Was kept in abject and disgraceful nonage.

TELL.

Unhappy man, thy uncle knew thee well,
When he withheld both land and subjects from thee;
Thou, by thy mad and desperate act hast set
A fearful seal upon his sage resolve.
Where are the bloody partners of thy crime?

DUKE JOHN.

Where'er the demon of revenge has borne them;
I have not seen them since the luckless deed.

TELL.

Know'st thou the empire's ban is out,—that thou
Art interdicted to thy friends, and given
An outlawed victim to thine enemies!

DUKE JOHN.

Therefore I shun all public thoroughfares,
And venture not to knock at any door—
I turn my footsteps to the wilds, and through
The mountains roam, a terror to myself.
From mine own self I shrink with horror back,
Should a chance brook reflect my ill-starred form.
If thou hast pity for a fellow-mortal——

[Falls down before him.

TELL.

Stand up, stand up!

DUKE JOHN.

　　　Not till thou shalt extend
Thy hand in promise of assistance to me.

TELL.

Can I assist thee? Can a sinful man?
Yet get thee up,—how black soe'er thy crime,
Thou art a man. I, too, am one. From Tell
Shall no one part uncomforted. I will
Do all that lies within my power.

137

DUKE JOHN (springs up and grasps him ardently by the hand).
     Oh, Tell,
You save me from the terrors of despair.

TELL.
Let go my hand! Thou must away. Thou canst not
Remain here undiscovered, and discovered
Thou canst not count on succor. Which way, then,
Wilt bend thy steps? Where dost thou hope to find
A place of rest?

DUKE JOHN.
    Alas! alas! I know not.

TELL.
Hear, then, what heaven suggested to my heart,
Thou must to Italy,—to Saint Peter's city,—
There cast thyself at the pope's feet,—confess
Thy guilt to him, and ease thy laden soul!

DUKE JOHN.
But will he not surrender me to vengeance!

TELL.
Whate'er he does receive as God's decree.

DUKE JOHN.
But how am I to reach that unknown land?
I have no knowledge of the way, and dare not
Attach myself to other travellers.

TELL.
I will describe the road, and mark me well
You must ascend, keeping along the Reuss,
Which from the mountains dashes wildly down.

DUKE JOHN (in alarm).
What! See the Reuss? The witness of my deed!

TELL.
The road you take lies through the river's gorge,
And many a cross proclaims where travellers
Have perished 'neath the avalanche's fall.

DUKE JOHN.

I have no fear for nature's terrors, so
I can appease the torments of my soul.

TELL.
At every cross kneel down and expiate
Your crime with burning penitential tears
And if you 'scape the perils of the pass,
And are not whelmed beneath the drifted snows
That from the frozen peaks come sweeping down,
You'll reach the bridge that hangs in drizzling spray;
Then if it yield not 'neath your heavy guilt,
When you have left it safely in your rear,
Before you frowns the gloomy Gate of Rocks,
Where never sun did shine. Proceed through this,
And you will reach a bright and gladsome vale.
Yet must you hurry on with hasty steps,
For in the haunts of peace you must not linger.

DUKE JOHN.
Oh, Rudolph, Rudolph, royal grandsire! thus
Thy grandson first sets foot within thy realms!

TELL.
Ascending still you gain the Gotthardt's heights,
On which the everlasting lakes repose,
That from the streams of heaven itself are fed,
There to the German soil you bid farewell;
And thence, with rapid course, another stream
Leads you to Italy, your promised land.

[Ranz des Vaches sounded on Alp-horns is heard without.

But I hear voices! Hence!

HEDWIG (hurrying in).
            Where art thou, Tell?
Our father comes, and in exulting bands
All the confederates approach.

DUKE JOHN (covering himself).
            Woe's me!
I dare not tarry 'mid this happiness!

TELL.
Go, dearest wife, and give this man to eat.
Spare not your bounty. For his road is long,

139

And one where shelter will be hard to find.
Quick! they approach.

HEDWIG.
 Who is he?

TELL.
  Do not ask
And when he quits thee, turn thine eyes away
That they may not behold the road he takes.

 [DUKE JOHN advances hastily towards TELL, but he beckons
 him aside and exit. When both have left the stage, the
 scene changes, and discloses in—

SCENE III.

The whole valley before TELL'S house, the heights which enclose
it occupied by peasants, grouped into tableaux. Some are seen
crossing a lofty bridge which crosses to the Sechen. WALTER
FURST with the two boys. WERNER and STAUFFACHER come forward.
Others throng after them. When TELL appears all receive him
with loud cheers.

ALL.
Long live brave Tell, our shield, our liberator.

 [While those in front are crowding round TELL and embracing him,
 RUDENZ and BERTHA appear. The former salutes the peasantry, the
 latter embraces HEDWIG. The music, from the mountains continues
 to play. When it has stopped, BERTHA steps into the centre of
 the crowd.

BERTHA.
Peasants! Confederates! Into your league
Receive me here that happily am the first
To find protection in the land of freedom.
To your brave hands I now intrust my rights.
Will you protect me as your citizen?

PEASANTS.
Ay, that we will, with life and fortune both!

140

BERTHA.
'Tis well! And to this youth I give my hand.
A free Swiss maiden to a free Swiss man!

RUDENZ.
And from this moment all my serfs are free!

[Music and the curtain falls.

Made in the USA
Middletown, DE
03 January 2023

21187748R00080